+++

LOST IN THE WASH WITH OTHER THINGS

+++

+++ STORIES FROM CHARLES NEVIN +++

+++ PUBLISHED BY APPLE ISLAND INK +++

CHARLES NEVIN has written for, among others, The Guardian, The Independent on Sunday, The Daily Telegraph, The Times, The Sunday Times and The New York Times. This is his first book of fiction, although he has published three books of non-fiction. The first, *Lancashire, Where Women Die of Love,* a paean to the neglected romance of his native county, was praised by Joanna Lumley, Jeremy Paxman and the Southport Visiter; Professor J K Walton, quondam Professor of Social History at the University of Central Lancashire, found it 'frivolous' but allowed it to be 'thought-provoking'. The second, *The Book of Jacks,* a history and lexicon of our most popular first name and the remarkable characters who have borne it, including his father and son, failed to achieve the success it deserved; indeed, a month after publication, the publisher said, 'It may be, Charles, that you and I are the only two people in the world who think this book is a good idea'. Charles still likes it. His third, *So Long Our Home,* a history of Knowsley Road, the famous old ground of St Helens Rugby Football Club, written with Alex Service, the club historian, is very popular in St Helens. He lives in an old watermill in Somerset just behind the railway station.

Published by Apple Island Ink 2016

A CIP catalogue record for this book is available from the British Library.

ISBN-13: 978-1530359493
ISBN-10: 153035949X

Produced by Craig Stevens
Cover design Liv O'Hanlon

+++ CONTENTS +++

'… for man is a giddy thing, and this is my conclusion.'
Benedick, Much Ado About Nothing, by William Shakespeare.

'It's red hot, mate. I hate to think of this sort of book getting in the wrong hands. As soon as I've finished this, I shall recommend they ban it.'
Tony Hancock, Hancock's Half-Hour, The Missing Page, by Ray Galton and Alan Simpson.

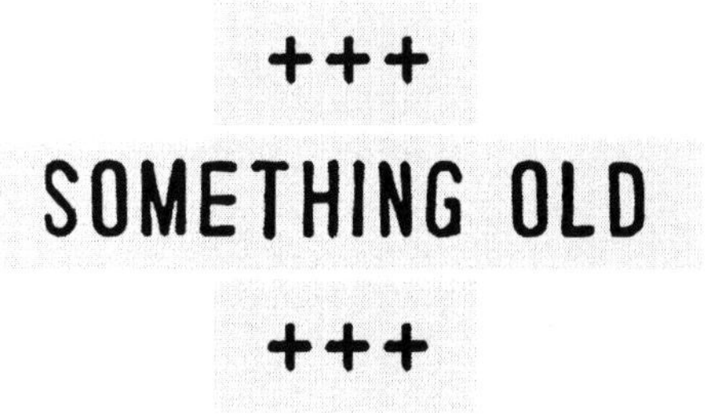
+++
SOMETHING OLD
+++

LOST IN THE WASH +++

DO YOU KNOW, I don't feel that good. Difficult to be sure, given the ghastly food you get in this country, but my bet would be on those peaches at Swineshead. Swineshead: what a charming name! Only a few rashers from Pigsbottom. Miserable, dank place. Another abbey. How many abbeys does one country need? I started off in one, but it was over the water at home, where at least the weather and the food are better, which wouldn't be difficult. Definitely the peaches, thought the custard was a bit dodgy at the time, too. Clearly curdled. Unusually duff for my personal chef, Walter, the wonderful Walter. Oh, but what am I saying: Walter wasn't there, was he?

Miserable and dank, but there was money somewhere, obviously, it being a monastery; but, equally obviously, not being too ostentatiously displayed towards Your Majesty, John, King of England. Wise move, as my chaps had been there before, and I'm always in need of a bit of the old, how you say, *largesse*. Especially now. If I had a bit more time, I'd dissolve all these monasteries. That would bring in a substantial increment to the Exchequer, all right. Pope would be a bit grumpy, but we have history anyway, even if we are presently as close as Saxon eyes. Chucked me out once, didn't do me that much harm. I was in the pig's stuff before, and I'm still in the pig's stuff now. Bloody hell. Might have been the pork, now I come to think of it, looked as if the monks hadn't cooked it long enough, mean knee-botherers. That would be a bit rich, I must say, as pork was the problem with my imaginative plan to offer the Emir of Morocco the conversion of England to Islam in return for some readies. Pig farmers wouldn't buy it. Truculent lot, the English, very little imagination, Norman or Saxon, rain's got to them. Not that the Emir was very keen, either.

Must have heard about the weather and the food, and the cunning ungrateful bastards who masquerade as the nobility over here. They didn't go for the Mecca master-stroke, either. Lots of grunting about crusades and batting for the other side; these people have absolutely no idea of the realities of global diplomacy or how much it takes to get back an empire and run a decent kitchen in such times as these.

MONKS, THOUGH. I could have been one. I had the Latin, but not the faith, and certainly not the patience. Pray, pray, pray, service, service, service, swing that thurible, shake that censer. I know a lot of people like the plainchant, but it's too much of a drone for me, I like some strings, the lute, as long as that old fool Blondel doesn't get anywhere near it. No wonder my brother recognised his playing when he was banged up in that Austrian castle, unique doesn't begin to cover it. Poor old Richard. How many gays are tone deaf? Exactly. Not very clever, either, the dead hero. Which was why he was in said chokey in the first place. How sensible was it to visit a Viennese brothel when you're supposed to be slipping back home incognito? I'm not entirely sure he knew where he was, either, especially as he complained to me later that the waitresses kept disappearing. And although it was very sporting and flashy to applaud that shot from the Chalus battlements, he should surely have remembered to get out of the way before it killed him. *And* he believed me when I told him that there had been a careless but crucial clerical error involving an unfortunate negative in the sentence in my letter offering the Holy Roman Emperor 80 grand not to let him go.

Still, he did forgive me, if rather condescendingly, if he'd known what that meant. And he had a stomach, a much better one than this feeble griping thing of mine. A stomach for a fight, and for food. Conquered by neither king nor kebab, but by his own impetuousness, Richard. Just another siege, the one at Chalus, boys toying; meaningless, really. Poor old Richard. But that's the trouble with fights: their tendency to be fatal, particularly given the current crude fashion for courage and the scandalous inadequacy of the armour. I prefer hunting: animals are rather more defenceless. And what on earth is the point of being leader if you can't take a strategic approach to risk, i.e. make your followers take it? We've had our differences, by one of his sanctimonious missives we have, but that's where the Pope and I are absolutely at one. You don't see him on a Crusade, do you? I said this to Richard once: he just laughed and said he couldn't hang about discussing brainy stuff, it was Wednesday and he was off to lay waste. But you won't see Your Majesty on one, I can tell you, even if I have promised Innocent I'll be on the Jerusalem tour as soon as I've sorted out this little local difficulty. No chance. The heat, my dear, and the people. Not that I haven't once more gingerly entered the breach from time to time, of course. But only when it's been entirely necessary, none of this ridiculous religious grandstanding or chivalry claptrap. John Softsword, they sneer, but no one calls me John Softhead, do they? And do you know, I've never been beaten in battle, never, even if they've been carefully selected appearances.

They all loved me at Mirebeau, the bold stroke to capture my snivelling little rebellious rival of a nephew, Arthur – who remembers him now? – and free my poor old mother from the castle where she had been so foully fettered. Even so, although I got my French possessions back, it could have gone rather better. Arthur, being a sadly typical teenager, showed absolutely no enthusiasm for fighting nobly to the death, and sulkily gave in, as they do, whatever. My dear mama, that conniving, cunning old she-wolf, showed her gratitude by refusing to connive and cun on my behalf and instead going off to a nunnery. Eleanor of Aquitaine: a nun?! How was I supposed to see that one coming? Story of my life – really bad luck. For yet another example, I never did discover which puddinghead got the exchange rate mixed up and made the bribes to kill Arthur so commercially unattractive. They said I did it with my own bare hands while drunk, but you can see my problem, especially after the lazy little feebling refused to take a turn round the battlements.

No sympathy from the monks, of course, which I couldn't give a fried-fig pastry for, except that they write the chronicles, the allegedly accurate historical accounts, you see. There's a Roger and a Ralph at it as I speak, in their comfortable monasteries, scratch-scratching away, and more bound to come, as the idle sods have bugger all else to do but bugger all they can get their sweaty hands on. And they've never liked me, for reasons already outlined, and more. That row over their choice for the new Canterbury is the obvious thing, but neither they nor we got the man we wanted, and I was the one who got excommunicated and the country interdicted before agreeing to that prisspot Langton, that great friend of the barons, that Becket worshipper, that Archbishoprick. Tried to stop my great reforms. And who's been censured now, eh, Stevie? Ask my new best friend, the Pope, finally persuaded by me that I am a sober, sensible, Christian king. Innocent is uninnocent, not a wholly holy fool, but he's not as clever as Your Majesty. That's what the chippy monks and prattling prelates hate. They know I've seen through them, the cant and the easy living and worse. My cleverness unsettles them, threatens their assumed monopoly on learning. Even the old saint himself, Hugh of Lincoln, was a bit wary, but I helped carry his coffin because he was a rare honest one. I came across him in his cloister one day when I was young and after the usual lectures he suddenly gripped me by the arm and said, 'Why are we here?'. I like a bit of doubt, it's intelligent and winning.

As for the rest of the knee-tremblers, I am magnificently untroubled by their self-serving mutterings about eternal damnation, pitchforks in sensitive places, turn over now and baste, as I'm clever enough neither to believe a word of it nor to show that I don't believe a word of it. This lot here won't be ready for an openly unbelieving king till the next millennium at least, if then. They do like some external blessing on their funny little offshore-island attention-seeking ways, like fighting and betraying their liege lord, the bastards. Still, they're Normans, aren't they, what can you expect? Semi-house-trained Vikings, and you know about them. Don't blame me, we married in, I'm a Plantagenet, an Angevin, from Anjou and the Loire, blessed by sweet grapes and a warmer earth, none of your long hours of rowing and all the rest of it for me, thank you. And don't get me started on the Saxons. Let's just say they're uninspiring company and ignore the problems with personal hygiene and the inconvenient fact that they're really Germans.

Anyway, be assured that the monks will be having a right old go at me in their barely literate outpourings. They've taken my carefully calculated gifts, the vestments, the alms, the foundation at Beaulieu, but has there been any sign of the expected *quid pro quo*: chronicles praising Your Majesty? Not a sniff of the old vellum. No Plantagenet has been more traduced and is likely to be unless he grows a hump or something. So thank you. Just to show there are hard feelings, I have indulged myself in one of my typically off-colour jokes by sending out free herrings to the nunneries. Don't get me started on them, either. Anyway, I now have my own chronicler, Robin of Locksley, loyal fellow with an eye for the target and telling phrase whose work will secure my place in history. We've just finished an exhaustive description of the tenacity and courage with which I forced through my human rights reforms in the teeth of reactionary feudal baronial resistance.

My stirring speech at Runnymede was particularly good: 'I am happy to join with you today in what will go down as the greatest demonstration for freedom in the history of our nation … I have a dream that one day all of you, my mighty subjects, will need no persuasion of the rightness of my deep conviction that we are all born free, free as the wind blows, as free as the grass grows, born free to follow our hearts. And that this freedom shall be forever inviolate except in certain specified circumstances that are laid out in the schedule available for inspection on request with notice after payment of a variable fee to be determined by the monarch or his assignees. Now let all go forward together mindful not of what the King can do for you but what you can do for the King, such as donating at least fifteen parts in every hundred of income'. I explained to Locksley that this was my 'robbing the rich to help the poor King' strategy. 'That's very good,' he said. 'I can use that.' I must see how he's getting on. We'll have to work out something exceptionally clever to cover the other day, though. Liquidating assets won't quite cut it, I suspect.

NO BETTER, probably worse. Sick in Sleaford. I'm spending so much time on the loo they should name it after me. Definitely the peaches. Bloody monks. I can still see the one who waited on us, and the fawning way he inquired, 'Just dessert, Sire?'.

Sleaford. Another terrible name, something to do with mud – Slea, slee. What a country. We have names like Fontreveau, Chinon, names that you can roll around your mouth like a good wine. Here they have Swineshead, Sleaford, Staines, Runnymede, and this disgusting Malmsey stuff. Have you tasted it? I know my dear bluff subjects over here find me far too continental, but, really. Good for nothing but drowning people in, I should have said. My sense of humour again.

Always getting me into trouble. But when you've had my luck and my life, you do need the odd laugh. Do you remember the time when that other old fraud, William Longchamp, Richard's man, the non-English speaking Lord Chancellor of England and Bishop of Ely – there's grand – was fleeing the country after his egregious arrogance and my various plots had done for him? The silly old fool had disguised himself as a woman and was assaulted by an over-amorous fisherman at Dover who soon discovered that Willy had a willy, so the game was up. By me, that was funny. It tickled me so much I let him get away to the continent. That's the thing, you see: I taught the English to laugh. I invented the English sense of humour, our marvellous mix of the broad and subtle. No laughs before me. Vikings, Saxons, Normans? Please. Have you read Beowulf? Or the rest of their absurdly violent and thumpingly obvious Sagas? I told you the Saxons were re-branded Germans.

I was old Eleanor's tenth, and I could sense that the experience had lost its novelty. I mean: John: how much thought and enthusiasm has gone into that name? Dad was a terrible old grump, so it did help if I could make him laugh, and, let's face it, there wasn't much else about, what with his revolting sons, that wife and the memory of that smarmy sanctimonious fop of a fraud Beckett always haunting him. Well, yes, I did a bit of revolting myself, but, come on, I am a Plantagenet, even if I am a little shorter, a little fatter and a little smarter than the rest. Well, all right, more than a little smarter. You read Locksley, it's all there. You don't come in from tenth by happy chance; such a lot of deaths. And you certainly don't get forgiven for treachery against your nearest and dearest, twice, or was it thrice, unless you have a certain *je ne sais quoi*, the charm that every short, fat, youngest son needs.

Ask my wives. Well, ask my second wife. Both were called Isabella, which simplified things and allowed me to recycle my witty pleasantry, Isabella necessity for a leper? I'm not sure

Isabella I appreciated it; between you and we she was not the sharpest wimple in the wardrobe. I married her for her castles and our issue was an issue as we were second cousins, and the Church gets very het up about matters sexual. Which is odd, on the face of it, for a spiritual organisation. The cynical might say this is because they aren't getting any themselves. The even more cynical, among whom we are proud to include Your Majesty, will point out that, as it happens, they're getting plenty. One of my better jokes during the late Interdiction was to take away the clergy's 'housekeepers' and charge for their return. My, they were cross, and, my, how much money did we make! I told you I'd introduced these dullards to humour, even if they show no signs of appreciating it. Still, I expect they'll be claiming they invented it, with no thanks to Your Majesty.

And what about that silly old fool of a hermit, Peter of Pontefract, with his prophecy that I wouldn't be king by next Ascension Day? I threw a big bash on the day and hanged him the next. And his son. Perhaps that was taking the joke a bit far. Anyway, how can a hermit have a son? Exactly. I'm not sure, now, too, about extracting money from that Jew in Bristol by extracting his teeth, one at a time, daily. Not perhaps the best way to repay the Jews for handing over most of the rest of their money in return for my protection. Actually, legally, I own them, which, *inter alia*, as we clever people say, means they can't own any property themselves: this enables me, in my brilliantly sneaky way, to acquire the land the numbskull nobility have put up in collateral for the money they've been lent by my Jews which the numbskulls usually can't repay, being spendthrift numbskulls. Perfect. But not entirely fair on the Jews, or their reputation, particularly given that they are by far the most interesting people to talk to round here. Nor am I convinced that my merry sally about pioneering state provision of free dental care was one of my finest.

But, like I said, I'm a Plantagenet. And I'm still here. Although I've felt better. Never mind, got to keep going, let me try you with another one: Isabella necessity for a church when the Pope has forbidden them to ring in an interdicted land? They didn't laugh at that one, either, dolts and dullards that they are. Isabella II did, though. I got rid of Isabella I over the cousin thing; at one stage they forbade me to have intercourse with her, which wasn't such a bad thing, I can tell you. But Isabella II! Isabella of Angouleme, the beautiful Isabella, a bewitching confection of honey, golden and dark, skin, eyes, hair, smell, breath, voice, everything, lending hot summer Provence to the earthy promise of an English May, a lavender shimmer to the apple sweetness, a warm breeze to the rough winds and the darling buds. And a wonderfully dirty laugh. May days: I can almost love this country on May days, when they stop grumbling, briefly, and caper merrily in their artless way in Spring time, the only pretty ring time. I took her off the dolt Lusignan, caused a war and lost it, but it was worth it. And as I said at the time, and often again as I lay long with her, there'll be time enough to win it all back. The English seemed shocked by this; they use all these wars, battles and skirmishes of theirs as both an excuse not to have sex and a substitute for it, you see, whereas, if I say it myself, I am the other way round, which is far too complex for them to get their Saxo-Norman heads round. If I'd insisted on finishing one of their silly games before taking on some fast approaching enemy they would have loved it, absolutely loved it. Instead I said I wanted to finish my game with Isabella and they all went red in that way of theirs, hopping from foot to foot. Must remind Locksley to mention that.

NEWARK, COLD and windy, and that's only me. I'm not finding riding that easy, what with the weakness and having to keep getting off. Still, things can only get better. I'll be as chipper as a pardoner with an apostle's wotsit in no time. It might look like I'm in a bad way, but I've been in worse places: have you been to Scarborough in February? No, they said I was finished when the returned Richard caught up with me in Normandy, but, as I said, he believed me when I explained to him at some length, with illustrations, that my actions had not been treachery but in fact a subtle triple bluff to outwit his enemies and preserve his kingdom, plus that clerical error which seemed to suggest I was offering to pay to keep him inside. I saw that familiar furrow appear on his brow, followed by the equally recognisable and stately arrival of a thought: 'Of course, dear boy,' he said, 'Now let's have some supper. Salmon tonight! And a particular treat for you – Blondel will play!' Happy days, even though I can see, and, sadly, hear, the old fool now, hand cupped over one ear, giving his caterwauling all to *Old York, Old York*. By us, I wish it was salmon tonight, no chance in Newark, the local delicacy here appears to be something unspeakable done to indeterminate intestines in a bread sauce. I'm glad I can't eat anything, frankly. What a tragedy we lost our poor Soxe in the Wash! What a treasure he was, that cook, Walter! The latest in a long line produced by the noted Soxe family of Sancerre, suppliers of superlatively succulent sauces and maskers of any amount of elderly inadequate ingredients. I think I could better have borne the Crown Jewels sinking below the waves.

But, as I said, when your luck's out, your luck's out, and the tide's in. Not great for Soxe, either, as it happened. Damned XXIV-hour-clock tide tables, we were completely at VI's and VII's, and then whoosh and Walter had gone and half our baggage with him. There's got to be a better system. That's what happened with Isabella II's age, too: some slack baldpate of a clerk left an x off, so she appears to have been twelve when we were married rather than 22. Probably reflecting his own monkish tastes. I've warned Innocent that it will get the Church in a lot of trouble one day. Must make sure Locksley's straightened that out. Where is Locksley?

WILL THIS RAIN never stop? A less determinedly optimistic man would be a bit down, feeling like death and a long way from home, from the smell of the thyme and the rosemary and the taste of some sun-warmed *Chaume* and the touch of Isabella. But she's at Corfe, down with the kids, nicely placed for the beach, even if it is October. Sundry other royal people, or threats, are down there, too, loosely imprisoned in a fairly fiendish device I'm rather proud of, the English holiday that's never over.

No, on the whole, I would not rather be in Newark. Still, this is the low point from which the truly great ruler recovers. I've failed again to recover all my continental possessions, thanks to some remarkable incompetence from my so-called allies, particularly my useless nephew of a Holy Roman Emperor, Otto, who somehow contrived to lose the decisive battle against the French that I had set up to avoid fighting one myself. My human rights reforms over here are being resisted by the particularly revolting Northern barons; the popinjay son of the French king is sashaying round the home counties like he owns them: and I'm having to whizz around up here like some Saxon with fleas to show I'm still a player. And I've lost my chef.

On the plus side, though, the barons who are frightened of me and the barons I bribe clearly represent, oh, let me see, LXVI.VI recurring per cent of the total, and they're not for shifting. I've taken in a fair amount of loot. The cock-up at the Wash could have been much worse. I'm a young, let me see, here we go again, XLIX-year-old, so there's plenty of time to get everything back. Well, yes, I suppose I would prefer mornings with Isabella, afternoons hunting, evenings a la carte and nights with Isabella, but all these lands, from even further north than this, from Bamburgh to Bastimente, from Dublin to the Dordogne, they belong to me, they're mine, and what we Plantagenets have, we do try to hold. And with me, you have to understand, it's personal, because by the time I was born there wasn't much left in the way of land for my father to hand out. John Lackland, they called me, which I didn't find funny then, and don't now, with this present passing shortage. It's not the principle of the thing, it's the money. The money comes with the land; when I lose land, I lose money, and then I have to extract more money from the land I have left to get the lost land back. I run an extremely efficient and imaginative pips-squeaking fiscal system, granted, but it's not really a satisfactory economic model, especially as a large part of the reason I lose the land in the first place is because I'm taking too much money and they side with my rivals and their empty promises of probity and moderation.

But, come on, this is the Middle Ages. We're not exactly talking liberal democracy. And there's a significant flaw in liberal democracy: no power for Your Majesty. And what sort of a system would pay us for doing nothing? Exactly. Never happen. Have you been to Dublin, by the way? My goodness, what exhausting people, heroic talkers, terrifying drinkers and dreamers, energetic if limited dancers, no arm movements to speak of, endless songs about wrongs and beauty, lot of it green. I rather got off on the wrong foot with them when my dad sent me to sort them out and I provoked a diplomatic incident by pulling the beard of one of their Chiefs. Actually, I thought it was an interestingly woven tweed scarf, but no matter, the effect was the same. It's sorted out now, however, after the same sort of show of strength and application of salutary violence that's also pacified Wales and those damn encroaching Scots. Future generations will hail me for solving all of that once and for all, if it isn't buried by the acclaim for my far-sighted founding of the Royal Navy and establishment of our hallowed island tradition of maritime *force majeure*, which the French will insist on calling state piracy for some reason, probably envy. Not bad, all this, eh? Worth a play, I should have said, if they can find anybody good enough to do me justice. But this is not the time to consider my legacy, there are lands to be gained, money to be made, deft deviousnesses to be delivered, fun to be had.

Everyone is looking a bit grave, though, I have to say. Locksley's just been and has assured me of the safety of the Crown Jewels, which he says he is looking after personally, and is keeping in a very safe place, not far away, but remote, which is reassuring. A touch vague, I thought, all the same, about our Chronicle. This besetting bug is make me very tired, and I do tend to drift in and out a bit, but I think he said that they were determined to find it, and were diving.

IT'S RIDICULOUS, but I seem to be dying. Fever won't go, food won't stay, can't drink enough, I can remember my energy but somehow can't seem to summon it. Doing the dreams and visions thing, too. Past coming back to me, not always in a good way. Can't rest, can't rise. No one dear near. Mercenaries, courtiers, same thing, can't even remember most of their names now. I'm too clever, too wary, to make good and true friends, always wanting something new, not clever at all, really. Haven't even been faithful always to Isabella, rather took the old *droit de seigneur* as a duty, I'm afraid. Hugged the children, but not enough. Not a good man; but not that bad a one, either, given the temptations, and the parents. One a saint-slayer and the other a man-eater. Sibling rivalry? Lack of cuddles? I'll be a case study one day. They tuck you up, your parents? Not mine, the reverse, similar spelling. Still, quite useful for a king, so young Henry should be all right. I'm getting maudlin now. Next I'll be summoning whichever monk might be creeping about in happy anticipation. I'm frightened, all right, frightened their heaven might turn out to be true. How much fun will that be? Anyway, the tonsured tosspots have already pronounced. Some superstitious nonsense about the Plantagenets being descended from a she-devil. Written by that dreadful old windbag, Gerald of Wales, and more widely advertised by another of them, Bernard of Clairvaux, founder of the Cistercians. 'From the devil they came, and to the devil they will return,' he said about us. Charming. Lots of Christian forgiveness and hope of salvation there. This from the man who sent thousands to their deaths after persuading them to go on crusade with about as much preparation as one of his sermons. My mother went on it, mad bat that she was, and much good it did her. Might just see you down there, then, Bernard.

WELL, THEY'VE BEEN about the last will and testament, I think. This pain is now so bad that I'm slipping away out of consciousness as much as I can, and I'm beginning to feel that soon I might not be able to slip back, especially if that jackanapes of a cook offers me the aforementioned speciality of the castle one more time. I told them my will was to be left alone and then I heard them talking among themselves about drafting the usual kind of thing, penitence, alms, God's will. Then one of them asked about the funeral arrangements and there was more wittering, including another rather disobligingly ruling out Westminster Abbey because they wouldn't be able to fill it. Bloody Londoners. They've always hated the way

I've encouraged other towns and cities. Liverpool, that's mine, terrific musicians there, by the way, Blondel. I don't want to be buried in England, anyway, thank you very much. No, I want to be taken back to Anjou, to Fontrevaud, to lie with my family as we lied to each other, to the safety of numbers. I doubt it will become a place of pilgrimage, although Isabella will obviously want to follow my mother into the nunnery. I tried to tell them it's to be Fontrevaud, but I can hardly concentrate now, let alone pronounce Fontrevaud. So I told them I wanted to be laid to rest where the sun is kinder, the grapes sweeter, the women prettier, the land finer, the food much better, ah, yes, the food, mouth watering meats, not watery mushes, complemented by the finest sauce in the world, produced by the incomparable Soxe family, had they tasted it, where was Walter, he could show them, they could taste it, oh, how I would like to for one last time, but the waters were rising, closing. I could hear myself blathering like this, but I could do nothing to stop it. They understood, I think; one of them repeated, 'buried … where they make…finest sauce in the world', looked puzzled, then nodded in sudden understanding and gave an order. It's getting darker, darker, fainter, and now John has smiled his last crooked smile and Lackland will lack land once again and finally. Don't pray for me.

John, King of England, Lord of Ireland, Duke of Normandy, Duke of Aquitaine, Count of Anjou, and Count of Mortain, died during the night of October 18 and 19, 1216 at Newark. His body was taken across England under the armed escort of his mercenaries to shuttered indifference and buried in Worcester Cathedral, reportedly at his request. His reputation is mostly based on the chronicles of three monks, the contemporary Ralph of Coggeshall and Roger of Wendover, and, perhaps the most persuasive, Matthew Paris, writing later in the 13th century. It's fair to say they were

not fans. Little else has survived. Similarly, no trace has ever been found or acknowledged of whatever was lost in the accident to the King's baggage train as it crossed one of the streams leading into the Wash while John made a more direct route between Wisbech and Swineshead on October 12. Jewellery never seen again included the imperial Holy Roman regalia of his grandmother, Matilda. There have been many attempts to locate the site of the disaster over the centuries; as far as I know, no one has thought to look in Sherwood Forest. John's son was crowned Henry III and reigned for 56 years. Isabella married Hugh, Count of Lusignan, the son of her thwarted suitor, giving him nine children to add to the five she had borne John. Stephen Langton's was the hand behind the elegantly monarch-muzzling clauses of the surviving versions of Magna Carta, earning him the censure of the conservative Pope Innocent; even so, he continued as Archbishop of Canterbury until his death in 1228. There is a pub named after him in Surrey. The last Plantagenet, Richard III, the Crouchback, lost his horse, his crown and his life at the Battle of Bosworth Field in 1485 and lay under a car park in Leicester until his recent rediscovery and burial in the cathedral there.

THE GREEN MAN +++

To those of a certain age, sex and disposition, there are few more enjoyable activities than an early evening in an English country pub accompanied only by two pints of bitter, a packet of salted peanuts and a good book. I am such a person, and this was such a pub, happened upon somewhere in deep Kent by a bold, satellite-unsanctioned diversion that had seemed a good idea at the time. How long ago exactly, I cannot remember, but the light seemed gentler and the mood more wistful, as it usually is in the past.

There were no guest beers, no blackboard, and no goat's cheese. There were exactly the right number of clientele, a small, mixed, cheery but not too loud group at the bar, a couple of couples at tables, and a few calm lone drinkers, enjoying their own pace and peace. The right number for me, but also the reason why most pubs have now shut. First pint of bitter acquired, I made my way to a table and wished the drinker nearest me a cheery good evening in a way I hoped suggested both friendliness and a firm intention to get on with my book, which in this particular case was *A Distant Mirror*, Barbara Tuchman's beadily brilliant survey of 'The Calamitous 14th Century'.

My neighbour was a lean, elderly man with those pale eyes that only the old have, the ones whose glisten may be to do with good humour, or just age. There was a suggestion of energy about him, though, there in the loose suit with the trousers going up almost to his chin, and the tufty, white, unruly hair. He smiled back at me and jabbed his finger at the Tuchman text. 'She's right about that,' he said. 'It was horrible here. Young kings, weak kings, greedy lords, stupid lords, famine, war, war, war and freezing cold, too. I expect you've heard of the mini ice-age we had, freeze the balls off a badger. No wonder the people revolted.'

To be honest, Barbara was in the middle of one of her worthy but fact-heavy backgrounders, the old boy seemed to know his stuff, and it would have been rude not to talk, even if I had been able to work out a way to do it politely. 'You're obviously familiar with the period,' I said, sounding to myself, familiarly, like a stilted condescending git. 'Yes, I am,' said the old man. 'My interest runs broadly from the Druids to Industrialisation. That's where it ends for me. Move away from the land and you're lost. You just end up working too much to earn the money to buy things you don't need. Chasing after beads and mirrors that will only reflect badly on you. I'd rather drink beer'.

I had a number of reactions to this. First was, yes, as I feared, probably a nutter. Engaging, folksy, bit of a twinkle, but, you know. It's a familiar pattern to a journalist, which is what I'm after being. Everything going normally, then suddenly it gets a bit weird. I was interviewing a man once who was earnest and cogent in his opposition to a planned development until an attractive girl passed and he suddenly shouted, 'Look at the tits on that!' He had with him an old and much creased plastic bag stuffed with papers and newspaper cuttings, another sign to the wary. This old man didn't seem to have a plastic bag, though; but he did have a beard, like a continuation of his white and tufty topping. My second thought was oh-oh, he wants a drink. But his glass was still pretty full, despite his sips from it. My third thought was that, actually, what he was saying was not without merit (hark at me). 'That's interesting,' I said. 'Have you heard of John Lloyd, the man behind *Blackadder, Spitting Image, The News Quiz?*' 'Comedy?' said the old man. 'Don't make me laugh. There's been nothing new since those two bastards Chaucer and Shakespeare were at it.'

He seemed unusually fierce against the two great fathers of our literature, so I asked him why. 'Funniest writers ever.

Merchants' sons, not toffs, too. But like all people who have anything to do with merchants, they were after advantage, the money. Chaucer served that treacherous swine, Richard II, the worst and weakest of kings; mad, they now say: bad, I say, and I know. Shakespeare was funny, the funniest, when he stuck to things happenings in forests. Snug, Snout and Bottom, what an act! But he wanted his bread buttered, too, that slippery son of a glover, and he didn't mind covering things up, applying the velvet, to get it. ' Jack paused, made some decision, then smiled at me and said, 'Tell me about John Lloyd.' Well: I'm not, as anyone will tell you, a man in need of second invitations. 'Lloyd has this theory which I remembered when you were talking about Industrialisation. He thinks that if Jung had been born when Newton was born and vice versa, we'd be much better off, as we would have had 300 years of psychology and only 100 years of technology, so we'd all be these sorted, centred, easy-going emotionally intelligent people who'd still be wandering around with horses and carts'.

'Quite interesting,' said the old man. '*Quite interesting*,' he repeated, when I still failed to register: '*QI*'. My penny finally dropped. 'Oh, I'm sorry, yes, very good, Quite Interesting, *QI*, Lloyd's quiz show.' Sometimes, as in this case with the old man, it's hard to tell whether a stare into the mid-distance is just a stare into the mid-distance or a registration of mild despair. He took another sip. 'Lloyd must live in the country, only place to think. Newton let the side down. He should have stuck with his magic, not got himself involved in the search for laws and certainty. How dull. Alchemy, that's the stuff, that was what he was really into, finding the Elixir of Life, even though it's slightly overrated, if you ask me, especially on a December morning. Life, I mean. Chaucer was a great dabbler, too. Jung might have been Swiss, but he knew the importance of dreams. Mind you, Newton did have his moments, you know.When he invented the cat flap, he made two openings in his laboratory door, one for his larger cat, and another for the smaller one. A Newtonian joke, I've always thought, but that's me'.

The old man smiled at me and I smiled back, while trying to think of something interesting to say. 'Ah, yes, the Swiss,' I said, a little tangentially, admittedly, but it was the best I could do. 'There's that great little speech by Orson Welles in *The Third Man*: "You know what the fellow said – in Italy, for thirty years under the Borgias, they had warfare, terror, murder, bloodshed, but they produced Michaelangelo, Leonardo Da Vinci and the Renaissance…In Switzerland, they had brotherly love, they had five hundred years of democracy and peace – and what did that produce? The cuckoo clock."' This is one of my party pieces, and I even attempt what I fancy is a touch of Harry Lime's elegant American accent. 'Graham Greene wrote it,' I said, adding helpfully, 'the novelist'. The old man smiled another of his smiles, both friendly and challenging at the same time. 'No, he didn't. Welles wrote it. They needed a bit of extra dialogue. "The fellow" was Whistler, who knew more about art than Switzerland, as it was full of some feared and ferocious soldiery at the time who might at a stretch have been kind to their brothers, but certainly weren't to anybody else.'

AS YOU MIGHT IMAGINE, I was reeling a bit now. I offered my new friend a drink, but he said he was fine, his glass was always half full. I smiled dutifully at his little joke and went up to the bar and ordered myself another. 'Fascinating chap,' I said to the man behind the bar, nodding towards the old man. 'That's Jack,' he said. 'He's been here for longer than anyone can remember. So long we often say they named the pub after him.' He shouted over to Jack, 'You *are* The Green Man, aren't you, Jack?' Jack smiled back, and took another sip.

'Don't tell me,' he said, with something between a snort and a guffaw, when I walked back with my pint, 'Dr Spooner once went to Greenwich looking for a pub called The Dull Man when he should have been in Dulwich looking for a pub called The Green Man.' Sadly, in every sense, it was true that I had been about to confide this gem, and to follow it up with the punchy extra that it was almost certainly apocryphal. 'It's apocryphal,' said the old man. I should have been put out and feeling a touch teased by now, but the old man's raillery was infectious, inviting me to join in the conspiracy against myself, and to delight in it, which I felt unusually disposed to do. Goodness, I thought, this beer is good.

'I'm something of an expert on the Green Man, as it happens, and not just here,' he said.

'I'll bet you are,' I said, getting more into the mood.

'The Green Man is not a man,' said Jack. 'He is a spirit but he is not supernatural. He is natural. He is nature. He is a symbol and he is himself. He has many names: Bacchus, Dionysus, Pan, Tlaloc and Kidr would be a few. He celebrates and is a celebration of when the Earth was young and enough; it was before thought, and it was fun. When you could abandon yourself without care of consequence, surrender yourself to your senses without the carping conscience of civilisation, reckless of your reactions or anybody else's, just jump.'

'Sounds like Glastonbury,' I said. 'A touch basic, all that open air, and ghastly when it rains. I've often wondered about the greenwood in the rain. Not so merrie, them, not much hey-nonny-nonnying then, I wouldn't have thought. And that's it, isn't it, surely? Like you said, before thought. And thought's done a lot for us, hasn't it? Produced beauty and knowledge and imagination and the comforts in which to produce them. Thought produced your beer.'

Jack snorted and took another sip. 'Beer is compensation for all the terrible companion developments thought's brought on, like work, cities, time and people telling you what to do. Most thought is fraud. The Greeks are hailed as the greatest thinkers, the pioneers of our so-called civilisation. And yet Greek mathematicians didn't acknowledge infinity. They feared it, tried to avoid it; it didn't suit the safe little fence or hedge they were trying to put round life. Such sophistication. Farming, crops, settling down, swopping exciting risk for dispiriting risk and endless work, they're the enemies of happiness and contentment. Better a dissatisfied Socrates than a satisfied pig, John Stuart Mill had it: you wouldn't think he'd ever seen a pig lying in mud and sunshine. Have you ever sat and stared at the sun on water or the moon under it without worrying you should be doing something else? That's what was lost. We lost. Lord what fools these mortals be!'

'That's Puck, isn't it?' I said, ' Is *A Midsummer Night's Dream* the only Shakespeare play you know?'

Jack laughed happily. 'Well, it's the one I like best, and the truest to himself, less of the Tudor-pandering, crude distortions and support for oppressive government you see so clearly in *Henry VI, Part 2.* The *Dream* is the truer, finer, gentler, inner Will, if you will. He was a man of Eden, or Arden, and that's why he went back.'

'Oh, come on,' I said, 'It wasn't all babbling of green fields for him, what about that property dealing and the law suits later on?'

'That wasn't him, that was Mistress Hathaway. What a pennygrinder! The best bed was far from the worst of it. A difficult woman. Will always said Lady Macbeth was a softer version.'

I looked at him to see if he was being serious, gave up in the face of so many lines and creases, and asked him. 'I'm Jack,' he said. 'It's difficult to be serious if your name is Jack. There's quite a history. Jack the Lad, edgy, cheeky chappy of the people, not beyond a bit of sharp practice, occasionally with an axe, as the giant discovered. A bit folksy, too, what with those fairy stories, moving into, whisper it, magic, Jack in the Green, back to the Green Man. Jack's very close to Bacchus, have you noticed? Close to our friend Puck, too, although not quite as keen on the special effects.'

Jack took another sip from his still half-full glass and winked. How are you with winks? Mostly, they're unsubtle, like an exclamation mark. Sometimes, they're delightfully conspiratorial (take a look, if you can, at Elizabeth Taylor's to camera in full Cleopatra fig). Others, like Jack's, deny the smile and challenge you to return the stare, which, in his case was deep and disturbing; my mind went back to phrases I'd read somewhere about the ancient tensions between settlement and wander, law and freedom: the threat from the forest: horns and shadows, the abyss of abandon, the Wild Hunt in full spectral cry. But it might have been the beer. 'No,' said Jack, 'I did have my serious moments, but that was all a long time ago. If you want a serious Jack, he's called John, or was until they started calling anybody Jack. They're laying up trouble, but, as I, or was it Puck, said, these mortals are fools and won't change much now.'

'What made you stop being serious?' I asked. He looked at me and said, 'I could tell you. But then I would have to kill you.' I smiled dutifully again. 'Very good, Jack, go on.' 'Go back, actually,' said Jack. 'To Barbara's calamitous 14th century. Over the Channel, first, to Beauvais, where the people were getting their usual hard time from the grasping so-called civilisers, the ones who want to be in charge, who want to be in charge of more and more land where and while other people, the so-called peasants, just want enough to have a simple but satisfying existence, with time to watch the sun on the water and the moon under it. Difficult, though, when the French and the English milords are indulging in their favourite sport, extreme hunting mixed with all-in jousting, war. Up and down the land they go, burning what they're not stealing. Don't ask where the intellectual stimulation might be, not wanted on voyage, just like a Bullingdon Club outing and nearly as violent.

'The Black Prince, that great hero, what a very bad man he was, the burner and pillager of them all, the indifferent murderer of the innocent many. Rule-breaker, ball-breaker, widow-maker. After Poitiers, which he won only thanks to that late charge by the turncoat Gascon, Grailly, there was more and more of it, and what wasn't taken by the English or their paid men was taken by the French nobles. So when the Dauphin, in addition to this, ordered the poor bloody people to start re-building the nobles' castles, it all kicked off.

'The Jacquerie – French peasants were all the same to the toffs and so all called Jacques – took up arms and burning and slaughtering as enthusiastically as their oppressors. Their leader, in a nice touch, was a man known as Jacques Bonhomme, the full condescending soubriquet for a pliant peasant. This Jacques turned out to have a great talent for tactics and organisation but less of a one for controlling his men. There were terrible things done, but that's what happens when you unleash the beast you've baited. And it ended when the chivalrous ones, the nobility, the gentry, note all those descriptions, came to face Bonhomme in battle. Nobody knows anything about Bonhomme now, and they knew little more then. But Jacques was a clever man; he knew his people's army was no match for the toffs in pitched battle, and he wanted to fall back on Paris and the support of the bourgeoisie, who for once had also risen off their fat bottoms. But his men wouldn't have it; they were mad as hell and wanted to fight.

'So he drew them up in English style, Crecy-style, Poitiers-style, with archers to the fore. The noble, gentle and chivalrous ones took fright at this and invited Bonhomme to talk. It was a trap, of course; and he knew it was a trap. But Jacques was a Jack: in the end, at the final reckoning, he couldn't resist a challenge, some sport. He didn't want to risk his men, but he was prepared to risk himself, because cocky Jacques always fancied his chances for himself. And as soon as he entered the lines of the chivalrous ones, the nobility, the gentry, of Charles of Navarre, pretender to all France, he was seized because the chivalrous ones, naturally, excluded anyone not like them. The army of Jacques collapsed at the news, massacre was done to them so thoroughly and horribly that their revolt was over for 400 years.'

Jack took another sip and stared at me. 'And what happened to Jacques?' I asked. 'Well, the chroniclers said that he was tortured and then beheaded. One account has him being crowned with a red-hot crown. But remember who wrote the history. Jean le Bel, nob; Jean de Venette, clergy; Froissart, romancer, chum of Chaucer. Who knows what really happened? A leader suddenly appears. Nobody knows anything about him, not even his age. They think they know his name, but do they know where he was from? Was he killed? Who was killed? How would they know? The important thing is that people thought he had been killed. And people wanted to think he had been killed. Good for fear, good for legend. The English version of Jacques Bonhomme, by the way, is Jack Goodfellow. And Puck's other name is Robin Goodfellow. And who do you think the Robin Hood fellow was?'

THE USUAL PUB background chatter continued. I hadn't noticed the muzak tape before; it was now playing Jimmy Dorsey and *Green Eyes*. My peanuts were finished, but, mad fool that I am, I didn't care. 'What do *you* think happened?' I asked Jack, who was enjoying his effect. 'I know what happened. Twenty years later, in Kent, not far from here, the people rose again, and marched again, because, yet again, the lords wanted yet more money to finance their incompetence and their wars. In 1381, they imposed the third poll tax in five years. Poll taxes, taxes per head, or community, have never been liked in England, because they fall equally and thus unequally on everybody, with far less of a sporting chance of avoidance, and the English do like their games. Plague, war, taxes and cold: the people suffered most of all. Worst, they were expected to pay for the purposes and pleasures of their soi-disant superiors, who salted the outrage by disdaining them rather than offering thanks for the forced subsidy to their incompetence and extravagance.' Jack was getting agitated, and the pub was beginning to listen.

'Jacques in France; Jack here. Most famous in those times, mostly because there's a pub called after him, was Jack Straw, even more shadowy than Jacques Bonhomme. Was he a leader, or a symbol of the Revolt, standing for all the people, the Jacks, who weren't going to take it any more?

I got to my feet. 'Hang on, Jack,' I said. The Gents was free of the usual hurricane hand drier, and there was a fine bit of grafitto at reading height above my stall. 'Question everything,' it read. Below it another hand had added, 'Why?' I went back to the bar, and, nodding to Jack, got in touch with my inner Bacchus by throwing caution to the wind and buying a third pint. I gestured to Jack; he shook his head and held up his glass, even though it now looked half empty. 'Whatever you do,' said the barman, 'don't get him on to William Walworth.'

'Jack,' I said, once I had sat down again, 'I can see your interest in your name, but aren't you making too much of a mystery out of all this? Jack was obviously a common nickname among the peasantry, and often used as an alias for obvious reasons, avoiding capture and all that unpleasantness with hot iron. Jack Straw was probably the alias for Wat Tyler – Tiler, straw, yes?'

Jack looked at me. He was smiling but his eyes had taken on the challenging otherness again. 'So now you're an expert, are you, Charles? Done a bit of reading and happy to impose comforting, apparently sensible explanations. Pretty clear whose side you would have been on when the honest men of Kent and Essex assembled at Smithfield to meet Richard, and our Wat galloped up to his king under the flag of parley and was struck down without warning, another example of the noble chivalry that had been visited upon Jacques those years before. You'll know who killed Wat, of course, Charles, being an expert.'

As it happened, I did; but I remembered the barman's warning about William Walworth, mayor of London, who has his statue at Holborn Viaduct despite stabbing the hero of the people to death. But that's London, notoriously unsentimental, and always given to following the money, of which the merchant Walworth had a lot. So I ignored Jack's sneer, and, emboldened by the bitter, tried a bit of goading back. 'The People hadn't exactly acquitted themselves with honour, though, had they? For example, they'd burnt down the Savoy palace of John of Gaunt, and the Temple next door, not to mention dragging the Archbishop of Canterbury out of the Tower and cutting his head off without so much as a by-your-leave. And just for good measure, the Lord High Treasurer too.'

'You weren't there,' said Jack. 'Honour? Honour!? You hadn't had these bastards condescending to you while robbing you. The Archbishop of Canterbury? He was the Lord Chancellor, too, the man behind the poll taxes. What kind of a priest is that? John Ball, he was a priest. I've no time for the usual religious guff, myself, but neither had John. A hedge priest, a priest of the road and the green and the cross, not the palace and the parlour and princes. What a leader! What a preacher!'

Jack's voice was rising, and, contrary to the usual crack in the chords of old men, getting stronger. I was still struggling to identify his accent, a mix of Eddie Grundy and David Attenborough and something more. The group at the bar smiled over indulgently. The muzak tape was now playing *Stardust*, sung by Hoagy Carmichael himself. 'You listen to what he said to the people when they came together, Kent and Essex, at Blackheath. You imagine staring down at London and wondering what you had done, and whether you would ever see home again. And then you hear this'.

Jack closed his eyes and loudly intoned the famous words:

'When Adam delved and Eve span, who was then the gentleman? From the beginning all men by nature were created alike, and our bondage or servitude came in by the unjust oppression of naughty men. For if God would have had any bondmen from the beginning, he would have appointed who should be bond, and who free. And therefore I exhort you to consider that now the time is come, appointed to us by God, in which ye may (if ye will) cast off the yoke of bondage and recover liberty.'

Have you ever heard a pub applaud? After perhaps a minute, Jack opened his eyes. 'What price your honour now? Forget the god-bothering, has anyone ever spoken better, truer? The chroniclers and the fancy historians might say those words are invented, but they weren't there, either, were they? So Gaunt lost his palace, some weak men lost their heads and the lawyers were thrown out of the Temple, and their books, their smooth and befuddling instruments of oppression, were burnt. It was no more than they deserved, and the people got nothing that they deserved but everything they expected, deep in their brave hearts. And John was hanged for it but Jack wasn't, no matter what they tried to say. Jack was still there twenty years later when King Richard was cast aside and was starved to death in Pontefract Castle like the people he had betrayed. Jack was still there 70 years later when Kent rose again. But haven't you got a warm, comfortable and civilised home to go to, Charles?' Jack was back teasing, less threatening. It felt like no one ever left The Green Man, and I certainly had no plans, not now the Muzak was playing *The Green Leaves of Summer*, the theme from *The Alamo*, which always makes me a touch emotional, all right, brings a tear to my eye, even if it does celebrate the loss of one group of colonisers to another in the struggle to take land that belonged to neither.

'You're weeping,' said Jack. 'And so would anyone who considers my sad tale. Now let's talk about the melancholy fate of Jack at his finest hour, when Jack Cade appeared with an angry army at his back and a real revolution, a real return to the good old days in his soul. God not in heaven, Jack got close! But not close enough, or I wouldn't be sitting here, humouring a cynic like you, for now.'

'GLAD TO SEE YOU'RE STANDING UP for yourself with this stranger, Jack. May I?' A a woman who could only be the landlady of The Green Man had already sat down with us before Jack gave her an entirely different smile. She was handsomely framed and tightly bound by a dress of green velvet which made a feature of her impressive frontage. The vividness of her carefully arranged blonde hair was matched by the assisted scarlet of her nails and lips and the bright stones in the rings on most of her fingers. Whatever she was drinking had a cocktail cherry in it, pierced by what looked like a small silver sword, but was probably just plastic. 'Your first time here is it, my darling?' she said to me, in an accent that was as pure London as Jack's was difficult to place. 'We don't get a lot of new faces in here, but the regulars have been coming for ages, haven't they, Jack?' 'Now don't start, Mrs Butshaw, I was just going to tell Charles here about Jack Cade.'

Mrs Butshaw smiled a smile that had as much of the faraway about it as is possible with a pub landlady. 'Ah, Jack,' she said. 'Man of mystery, knave of hearts. No one knew who he was or where he had come from, and he certainly wasn't clear about it, was he, Jack? Some said he was from Kent, but was he? Have you heard of Jack o' Kent, another man of myth, hailing from the Welsh Marches, friend of the great Glyndwr, the last and lost true Prince of Wales? Some say he *was* Glyndwr. Whatever, both of them disappeared about 40 years before Jack Cade appeared. If Jack was pressed too much, he used to say he was a Mortimer, but no one really believed him, because the Mortimers were toffs, related to royalty and Jack was no toff, was he, Jack?' Jack smiled again. 'Still I suppose it suited his purpose. And he did look rather lordly, tall, with clear green eyes and the fiercest charm. Think Russell Brand, but a Russell Brand who would kill you. He certainly won the heart and more of the landlady of the White Hart in Southwark, where he made his headquarters when the rebels got to London. She thought he was the finest thing to come her way in a long time, not such a surprise when you consider the dull little geezer of a mine hoste she was married to.' Mrs Butshaw shot a glance towards the barman, who was very methodically polishing glasses while whistling along to the Mel Tormé version of *On Green Dolphin Street*.

'Blimey,' I said, attempting some vernacular myself. 'You seem to know even more about it than Jack. Is this a pub only open to medieval historians?' Mrs Butshaw gave me a look which I recognised from vain attempts to be served after the final bell in the days when licensing hours were stricter and I was younger: pleasant but distant. 'Oh, I don't know about that, Charles,' she said. 'We certainly like to remember the olden days, though, don't we, Jack? When we felt really alive. When our Jack was Lord of London!'

Jack was back there, too, now. He was more upright, the trousers had retreated to his waist, and his hands, large but elegant, were placed palm-down on the table in front of him. It would be fanciful, even for me, to say that he seemed in a trance, but his voice had certainly taken on a timbre and cadence I hadn't noticed up till now, and, wherever he was in his mind, it wasn't The Green Man, where the muzak had moved on to *Distant Drums*, by Jim Reeves. 'Oh, yes,' he said, 'Oh, yes. No one else seems ever to have remembered this, inconvenient probably, but when the people gathered once again at Blackheath, once again from Kent and Essex, 70 years and no further on in their fight to take care of themselves, Jack fizzed them up, like any good general, with that speech by John Ball, even including the God bits. They were ready after that, how ready! Have you ever been in a crowd walking towards the big game, or stood and watched a carnival procession go by? That was how it was, down into London, following Jack, on that summer's day, bringing the country to the city, fresh to the fetid, ready to blow. You could feel the power, the thrill and the purpose. And you could feel the faith in Jack: Jack Amend All, come from out of the greenwood to put things right, the rule of nature before the rule of law, a touch of Jack, a touch of the old magic, the old Jack magic. Forget crafty Will Shakespeare's cunning portrayal of Jack as an agent of conspiring nobility against the Crown: Jack is and always was completely out of control. That's Jack's point. Down they went into Southwark, where Jack, who's always loved a pub, chose The White Hart as his headquarters. Some say this was revenge on King Richard, whose sign it was. But I wouldn't neglect the landlady, very comely in the way of the very best landladies.' Jack looked at Mrs Butshaw, who, if she had been the blushing sort, would have, but instead gave him a fond, amused look.

'It was all going so well. Most of London was as fed up with the hopeless and hopelessly corrupt ruling class as the men from the country were. After a very lively night at The White Hart [another glance at Mrs Butshaw, reciprocated], Jack led the way over Southwark Bridge. The King had dithered, advanced and departed, the great City was there for the taking, and Jack took it. Imagine how it was: the old ways, the green ways, in a triumphant takeover of the rogues, robbers, cowards, cuthroats, mainchancers, betrayers, haters, all soiled by the dirty city, yes, the naughty men, cowed by the power of the upbraiding memory of a better, simpler way. And Jack, ever the showman, the illusionist, saw his chance to strike it home. He took his staff, symbol of the forest, from the forest, and smote the London Stone, some piece of foppish Romano masonry that happened to be in the right place at the right time, and declared himself 'Lord of London!'

I tried to be clever, again. Or it might have been the beer. 'It sounds just like Nigel Farage after a UKIP by-election victory,' I said. 'Pub, press conference, gesture.' I hope you are not as familiar as I am with the sally that falls flat, for want of timing, or just wit. Mrs Butshaw maintained the distant smile, Jack ignored me; they were both somewhere else. 'That was the best of it, really,' he said. 'The crowd, as they say, went wild. But that was what they were supposed to do. Blow away the sham and deceit that passed for progress and sophistication, rip it up, root and branch. And who had the axe? Jack!'

I looked into Jack's eyes and I saw again the deep pools of another, older world, felt the thrill and threat of chaos and abandon. 'Oh, yes,' he said. 'When you call on Jack, you don't get just the sharpness and the wit and the daring. You get the full force of what you're trying to defend. And what's that, Charles? It's freedom. And freedom isn't only freedom to do what you might mimsily call good things. No, you get Jack in full cry. So, Jack might have called on his followers to behave, but he didn't believe it or in it. So, on Saturday, July 4, 1450, after he'd called for the worst of the malign incompetents to be handed over, he had the chief money man, Lord Saye, the Treasurer, despoiler and grabber of the Cinque ports while he held travesty of local office, beheaded in front of the new fountain in Cheapside, and his head and the heads of a further few choice bastards mounted on spears. And then Jack dragged the headless naked body of Saye behind his horse through the City and back into Southwark. Well, you can see what happened: the crowd went wilder. The wild hunt was loose. Londoners began to realise what they'd done by letting Jack in. Another few days and there would have been no London, which would have suited Jack fine. You might have wondered, Charles, about that name, Cade. It's cod, mocking Latin, a dig at the first so-called civilisers of these islands. From 'caedere', to kill. Jack the Killer. Has a ring to it, doesn't it?'

I was beginning to feel very uncomfortable. The muzak was now *The Green Green Grass of Home,* which I'd never found unsettling before, even if it is about a man about to be executed dreaming of being laid to rest beneath the title. 'The trouble with riot, abandon and anarchy,' Jack was saying, 'is that it is riotous, abandoned and anarchic, and thus at the mercy of any half-organised force, especially one fighting for its life. Jack and his men were far too disturbing for the Londoners, who drove them back into Southwark. When the wavering country folk, now a little worried by Jack, too, were offered a pardon, it was all over. They had found Jack too rich for them. They wanted to mix and match the wood with the plough, freedom with fetter, license with licence. They didn't want liberty, they wanted a defined, protected liberty, which was and is far too complicated for Jack. He disappeared again.'

'I thought Jack the Killer was killed himself, back in Kent,' I said. This produced the first smile from Jack for some time. 'They killed a man they said was Jack. Why wouldn't they, when there was a reward of 1,000 marks? They brought a body back to The White Hart, where it was identified as Jack by the landlady. And why shouldn't she, when she would be happy to see Jack given a life alibi, even if they hadn't offered her 1000 marks?' Mrs Butshaw's smile became even more distant, six centuries away. The barman was still polishing the glasses. 'What did happen to Jack, then?' I asked.

'Jack stayed around,' said Jack. 'But I knew my moment had gone. A decision had been made, and I was on the wrong side of it. England chose a botched, muddled moderation. Oh, there were times when matters seemed to be moving my way, but I knew they weren't, really. The Tudors had a clever mix of power and myth that the Stuarts didn't understand, and the Civil War promised a review and return to me. But there was too much worthiness, even in the anger, too much Christ. Christ did for Jack. Plutarch has the story of the Aegean helmsman during the reign of Tiberius who heard the loud cry one evening, 'The Great God Pan is dead!'. That was the moment of Christ's resurrection. It's been the same for Jack, it just took longer. The Levellers, the Muggletonians, all the Puritans, looking back to the land, yes, but, Christ, again, they were dull! So poor Jack became a sorry symbol of the opposite, some cosy concoction of May and posies and poles and vaguely arboricultural cavorting, of some sort of safe fun. Bad Jack was mostly confined to the odd pirate, outlaw or serial killer, or to one half, like John Wilkes, the great reformer and people-mover and equality-demander, known as Jack when he was being radical or racy, but always destined to be defeated by convention, and to accept it. Do you remember what he replied when he was an old man and a woman of the same age hailed him on the street with the old cry, "Wilkes and Liberty!"? "Shut up, you old fool," he said. "That was all over long ago."'

Jack took a sip from his glass, which was now almost empty. 'And that's how I feel,' he said. 'I knew it was finally over for me when the Great War of 1914-18 industrialised the killing of millions and their dreams in terrible, mocking, muddy hauntings of fields and woods, all green gone. Kipling lost his son in it, the son he had urged to go to it. His epitaph will do for me, too: "Have you news of my boy Jack? Not on this tide".'

MRS BUTSHAW WAS MOIST-EYED, and, like any good landlady, cross with herself for it. 'Another drink?' I asked them. 'I think you've had enough, Charles,' said Mrs Butshaw. 'Charles,' said Jack, 'You've got to go. Not Jack enough. Bit of a know-all. And a terrible sense of humour.' 'Charles,' said Mrs Butshaw, 'You're barred.' The muzak was now playing *Some Enchanted Evening*, from the film of *South Pacific*, Rozanno Brazzi dubbed by Giorgio Tozzi. Jack was staring at me again, with that smile. The walls of The Green Man were fading as Jack came closer. I could smell him, a combination of leafmould, well seasoned hippy, the aniseed you used to get from gobstoppers, wood smoke and something so musky it should have been horrible but wasn't. Jack was looking much younger now, and beginning to fit Mrs Butshaw's description of the Lord of London, but more animal, more shaman, more bosky. Have you ever dreamt you were naked in public? Have you ever been naked in public? I felt like that. And then Jack hugged me, and I swooned. Visions followed of Pan, Jack and Mrs Butshaw doing something extraordinary with each other while somehow all smiling challengingly at me to a mix of Brazzi/Tozzi and, to be frank, a rather clichéd combination of pipes, horns, discordant brass, grunts and cries.

When I came to, I appeared to be halfway through a half of lager. The pub was busier, mostly serving food, including goat's cheese. The patrons, whether accompanied or not, were engaged in the usual i-down at their mobile phones. It all felt rather reassuring. Jack might never have been there. Mrs Butshaw wasn't either. I fished my own phone out and Googled several topics, including The White Hart, Plutarch, and the lyrics to The Green Green Grass of Home. I stopped when I read that there had been two plugged holes of different sizes in the door, now lost, of Isaac Newton's old Cambridge rooms, and that Jacques Bonhomme was the alias of a man called Cale. I could find no comment on the coincidence of Cale and

Cade, separated by a consonant and 100 years. Even Barbara was silent. I picked her up and left, and after some difficulty achieved the celebrated certainties of Tunbridge Wells. All in all, after all, I think I'm better suited to The Dull Man.

With apologies to, and much admiration for, Geoffrey Chaucer, William Shakespeare, William Morris, Rudyard Kipling, George Orwell and Claude 'Curly' Putman, Jr.

+++
SOMETHING NEW
+++

LOOKS LIKE CARELESSNESS +++

Jackson wasn't listening to the Today programme. It was the so-called 'light item' that they tended to spin out mercilessly until nine o'clock, something about beards. Moving slowly in the traffic towards his office, he had grown tired of just gloomily staring and was now aimlessly pondering. Bloody traffic. The 2-0 loss to Arsenal hadn't done them any favours, just when they seemed to running into a bit of form. How will Mum be on Saturday? Why do people insist on using 'less' when they mean 'fewer'? Sarah's been a bit odd, a bit distant lately. Why is everybody 'special', 'passionate' and 'on a journey'? Why do academics insist on using the present tense to talk about the past? Why is Simon Jones such a crashingly supremely irritating pompous fart? He changed the radio to the CD, which, as usual, was playing Led Zeppelin, Robert Plant on full scream.

Arriving at last, he drew into the car park and parked in the space marked with the number plate of his last car, the dull old Saab he'd finally and reluctantly parted with after the argument with the electric gates as he was leaving the cocktail party Simon Jones insisted on throwing annually. Jones was the only person Jackson knew still throwing cocktail parties, just as he seemed to be the only senior partner anywhere who hadn't noticed that even footballers were wearing cutaway collars now. Prat. He got out, just resisting the impulse to slam the door of his sensible sensible something or other into Jones's irritatingly white Mercedes in the next bay. God, he thought, I'll be running my key down its side soon, just a pity about the CCTV.

Inside, he sat down and resumed conveyancing. This concentrated on the crucial question of whether his client, the vendor, should insure the purchaser against the possible consequences of alleged badger activity near the wall between the property and the adjoining garden. Jackson sighed. It wasn't as if he had failed to fulfil early promise; this was precisely what his tutor had predicted for him, give or take the badgers. True, there had been that chance to go to Hong Kong in his thirties, but he was quite relieved when Sarah wasn't keen to sacrifice her dentistry practice. Apart from that, not much else, really, steady career, small town, two grown-up children, boy and girl, more interested in London than them. There was that occasional thought that he wasn't more of a success, that much of his annoyance with Jones might be because he wasn't the senior partner instead; but, like the rest of him, it was a polite thought that wouldn't dream of nagging. And, again, as with Hong Kong, any regret at failing to find his passion was overruled by relief that he hadn't had to commit himself. But Jackson was what used to be called 'a nice chap'. He cared about his family, his clients, even the badgers. And his mother was a worry.

Once, parents would do their best, ask for nothing in return, then shuffle off with minimum fuss when no longer required. True, there had been some bad hats, some who were less than duly diligent in the doing-best department, some attention-seekers and some hangers-on, but by and large it had worked rather well. Now, though, hanging-on was the norm. Medicine's random successes and failures had brought longer life for the body but not the mind. Now, across the country, hidden behind the walls of countless large old houses approximately converted for the purpose, countless mindless old bodies were purposelessly being kept alive by countless pills and procedures because nobody knew what else to do with them. Well, that wasn't quite true: because nobody knew what else to do with them that didn't involve killing them.

Jackson's mum, Jilly, was one such. Alzheimer's, naturally. She was 89. Jackson had been through the familiar decisions: when she could no longer live on her own (Jackson's dad had died some 20 years before), his wife, Sarah, had suggested they might look after her at their home. But the practicalities, and particularly the expense, made this a less and less attractive prospect, as they guiltily conceded first to themselves then to each other. After a dispiriting traipse round any number of homes, they agreed on minimum requirements: that it didn't smell of warm cabbage and that it didn't smell of warm urine, either. Autumn Leaves House was better than that but nonetheless, like all the rest, the television and the determinedly jolly carers were too loud, as if the noise could somehow drown out why they were all there, sitting and staring; rather like him, Jackson thought with a smile-grimace. Must get on with the badgers.

He hated his weekly visit to the Autumn Leaves EMI unit. The initials euphemised what they stood for: Elderly Mental Infirm, requiring a locked door on the unit and close attention lest they wandered off or worse. Jilly, summoned from her stupor, always knew him, although sometimes she thought he was his dad, or hers. Her eyes would light with pleasure, to be quickly followed by an intense, almost awed, recall of the horror that had happened to her: '*Oh, Philip!*' Conversation such as it was with what was left of her was confined to haphazard memories, often prompted by photographs, the more painful for Jackson for the faces she couldn't remember. The thief of an illness had spared her sense of humour, but sharpened it. Once, faltering to fill the lengthening gaps, he had pointed to his shoes. 'New,' he said. Previously, this news item would have been hailed like all his others as miraculously unique. 'Not that interesting,' she said now, as a calm statement of fact, an aside, to someone who wasn't there, perhaps herself.

But that was much easier to take than her surroundings. No amount of loud cheerfulness could disguise why the EMI patients were there, nor their pitiable condition: Irene, walking, muttering, always worried, back and forth, back and forth, advancing only on her end; May, with the rising repeated scream which changed, possibly in his head, from 'Waah!' to 'Woe!' and sometimes 'Why?'; June, singing gruff and word-perfect to the cheap tunes that were all she had to cling to; silent Ann, with her face of frozen fear; Rita, blank, able only to react, only to smile or scowl, depending on whether it was Irene or June. Others, either asleep or asleep even when awake, were locked in but out of themselves, ghosts already. After his visit, Jackson would go for a walk, guiltily relieved, half-stunned by the hopelessness of it.

EVERY YEAR or so his friend Mark Percival would ring, suggesting that they go and have dinner at their old college. Jackson and Mark had been at school together and gone up together. Afterwards, Jackson had gone back, but Mark had left for London and a career as a journalist turned novelist; he was currently having some success with his series featuring Saul Pinewood, the troubled baker and detective. Jackson was not over-fond of wearing black tie and going to hall for a formal dinner, but he did enjoy the way it peeved Simon Jones, who had been to somewhere less distinguished which Jackson always affected not to remember. Besides, he liked Percival and was finding fewer and fewer people to like as he got older and the more unattractive foibles of friends – dullness, success – began to overwhelm the others. Sarah encouraged him to go, which he put down to her eagerness not to be part of any meeting with Mark, whose friendship with Jackson was far too exclusive for her taste.

After the usual sherried small talk in the Senior Common Room, he took his place in the remembered old hall at the top table, satisfyingly raised above the long rows of present students, who looked less scruffy, and interesting, than his intake. He was between two fellows, his old law tutor, James Roby, and Travis Burns, an elderly medievalist. Memories of harrowing tutorials and the unimpressed verdict on his future had left him uneasy with Roby, who, after a clearly judgmental silence, asked him, 'Any decent cases recently?' Jackson decided on a bit of embroidery. 'Badgers,' he said. 'Fascinating business. Burrowed their way from my client's garden into next door's. A big one chased the neighbour into his house. The terrified man locked himself in the loo. For a while he could hear the badger breathing heavily on the other side of the door, then silence. When he finally dared to come out, the badger was gone but there was a large steaming turd in his drawing room pot pourri.' Jackson was aghast at himself but not a little impressed, even though he had dismissed his original thought of the badger being caught red-pawed raiding the fridge.

Roby was looking at him with what could have been new respect. 'Remarkable,' he said. 'It has elements of Lomax v Makinson, 1892, but that was a pig, and hinged on a gate.' As in many a tutorial, Jackson nodded his head wisely at this although he had no idea what Roby was talking about. He was saved by Travis Burns taking an interest. 'Funny thing about pigs. Their penises are shaped like corkscrews, right hand thread. I seem to remember that Robert Herrick had a pet pig which he taught to drink from a tankard, but don't quote me as of course I die in 1500.' Jackson and Burns spent the rest of the dinner mostly before 1500, with occasional excursions into how to put a pig into a trance and how Oxford had always been not what it was. Roby talked mostly to Mark on his right; from time to time. Jackson felt Roby staring at him, but he felt buoyed rather than concerned. 'I really must do this more often,' he thought to himself, moving the conversation on to Arthurian legends, always something of an interest, particularly the contention that the great warrior had fought several battles near Wigan.

After dinner, Mark and Jackson moved together over the port. There was the usual comfortable but inconsequential chaff between old friends about family and the past. What was noticeable now was that the hot topic was no longer their children but their parents. Mark's chief complaint was the behaviour of his father. 'My god, you wouldn't believe the amount of money he gets through,' said Mark.

'I thought he was the shy and retiring type of retired local government officer,' said Jackson.

'But that's it,' returned Mark. 'It's like he's been storing up for most of his life, and now he's gone mad. He even makes jokes. And the money! I don't know where it all goes. Well, actually, I do. On horses and drink, and, I'm ashamed to say for some reason, women. And then there's the flash car. My dear mum used to keep him in check, but since she's been gone, he's been completely out of control.'

'Women?' asked Jackson, as they'd both known he would.

'Oh, yes, it's ghastly,' said Mark. 'Hard-faced good-time girls with their good times well behind them. You know the type, too blonde, too loud, strangely immobile features, eyebrows go up when they sit down, that sort of thing. And Dad's a scream and I'm just the boring disapproving son who's no fun. The current one's a frightful creature called Tracy with a laugh like a ringtone and eye shadow the colour of a Russian's basement swimming pool. She'll marry him if we're not careful. I keep telling her there's no money but she thinks quite rightly that I'm trying to put her off. But there isn't any money.'

'So where's it coming from?' asked Jackson. 'From me and from payday loans and then me when he can't pay them. He does have the occasional winner on the horses, but that just encourages him to lose more.'

'Can't you just refuse to give him any?'

'He's my dad, Jackson. He bailed me out of a few spots when I was young. And what would happen to him? It's too terrible to think about.'

'What about a stern lecture, tell him he's embarrassing himself and everybody else. Tell him he's hurting you.'

'Yeah, that just what he used to say to me, and remember how successful that was. You've no idea what it's like trying to do it in reverse. I just can't stop listening to myself and thinking, "Christ, what a pompous arse you are, Mark." I wasn't very good at it with the kids, so this is hopeless. You were lucky, your dad was a responsible bloke, wasn't he, Jackson? Bit dull but at least he knew how to behave. Not like Arthur Bloody Percival, last of the red hot buggers. How's your mum?'

Jackson felt a tug of loyalty to his father, who had known how to behave too well. Jackson sometimes blamed his father for handing him the same trait because it was easier than blaming himself. 'Oh, Dad had his moments, you know,' he said, although he hadn't. 'It's pretty bloody with Mum, actually, Mark. I'm getting to the stage where I absolutely dread going to see her. Every Saturday, fear, confusion or a void from her, despair for me.' He went on with an edited version of his and her troubles, but less edited than it would have been without the port.

They moved back to the Senior Common Room, where Burns, Roby and the other fellows soon made their farewells, muttering various familiar saws and couplets, except Roby, who wanted Jackson to 'keep him up to speed' on the badger.

'How's the great Saul Pinewood?' asked Jackson, as they lingered. 'Working on one at the moment?'

'Saul's been very good to me,' said Mark. 'He does sell well. People seem to enjoy someone who can solve crimes while whipping up a windtorte.'

'I loved the last one,' said Jackson. 'Brilliant twist with the undercooked Fruity Swedish Tea Ring, the half-open window and the anaphylactic chauffeur with a past.'

'Thanks. I enjoy working out the plots.'

'So, to ask the famous question, how do you get your ideas?'

'Well, to give the famous answer, they're all around, just waiting to be used. I mean, take what we were just talking about – my dad and your mum. Perfect for a Strangers-on-a-Train-type scenario, isn't it?'

'A Strangers-on-a-Train-type scenario? Hold on to your hyphens, Mark. You're talking to a small-town solicitor, not one of your black-clad coffee-clutching media chums-in-a-hurry.'

'Come on, Jackson. I've known you a long time, remember. Don't come over all Atticus Finch on me. *Strangers on a Train*, the Hitchcock movie, the Patricia Highsmith book. Two strangers meet on a train and agree to swop murders so there'll be no detectable motive.'

'Yes? And? My mum and your dad? How does that work?'

'Too much port, Jackson. Simple. In the fictional world, I would murder your mum and you would murder my dad. We couldn't bring ourselves to do it to our own parents, but a friend would do it for a friend. Actually, the more I think about it, the better a plot it gets. Friendship, love, parents, children, agonising modern dilemmas, truth, relevance, inspired re-working of Highsmith. Could be a Booker in it, but not perhaps with Saul Pinewood, there'd be enough without a depressed baker. This could be the big serious one.'

'Crikey, it really is a different world, isn't it?' said Jackson. 'These are our parents you're talking about, you know.'

'Yes, yes, I know. I'm not seriously suggesting it, obviously. But, come on, don't be stuffy, it's an intriguing thought, isn't it?'

Jackson was quite surprised by the strength of his reaction to Mark's idle plotting; he recognised this was because part of him, rather than immediately rejecting the idea, had been quite attracted to it, and that this part of him was not a part he liked. Still, it was obviously the stuff of fiction, and, in any case, Mark had moved on and was now discussing his chances of winning the Booker now they'd let the bloody Americans in. Jackson didn't think he had ever had a bachelor's chance in Jane Austen, frankly, but fortunately it's not the function of friends to fracture dreams; that's best left to those even closer, like family.

They parted for the night, several hours earlier than of old, after another lap of the past and some perfunctory duty-mentioning of children and wives (in Mark's case, former wife: Maggie was now living on a houseboat with their equally former landscape gardener, a snake, or rather rake, in the grass called Bernard Charnock). As they parted, Jackson, again rather to his surprise, found himself telling Mark that he would go and see his father: 'Let me give him the responsibility lecture. I'm a solicitor, we're good at the pompous stuff, it's what we do.' Mark went through the usual English no-that-would-be-too-much-couldn't-possibly-expect-you-to-do-that-well-if-you're-sure-it-would-be-absolutely-terrific-but-only-if-you-are-absolutely-sure-I-am-at-my-wits'-end-you're-a-pal-Jackson-let-me-write-down-his-telephone-number-but-no-obligation-you-understand gavotte but was clearly quite touched and relieved by the offer.

LATER THAT week, after some more badgering – his opposite number was concerned about whether the waiver would cover one badger sett or all – Jackson called Arthur Percival. 'Well, as I live and breathe, it's Jack Jackson. How's it hanging, old boy?' It was mid-morning, but Jackson suspected that Arthur was not entirely sober. He was also talking to someone else with him. 'Not now, sweetie…ooh, cheeky sweetie!…now what do you want, Jackson? That priggish son of mine has put you on to me, hasn't he? He seems determined to stop me having the fun I deserve… sweetie, stop it, I'm talking to a friend of Mark's … yes, yes, sweetie, but he means well, even if he is a bit envious, and he is my son … sorry, Jackson, where were we? Haven't got long, off to the races, why don't you come, I need a bit of subbing, nothing too much, just to get me going properly.'

Jackson, possibly thrown by the new Arthur Percival, a previously shy and stuffy presence, and definitely unseized by the outlook at his desk for rest of the day, agreed almost without hesitation. 'Excellent. See you at 1.30 by Gentleman Jim's.' 'Gentleman Jim's?' asked Jackson, who was not a regular racegoer, despite the local course's attractions. 'You're not a regular racegoer, are you, Jackson?' said Arthur. 'Gentleman Jim Murphy, on-course bookmaker about halfway along. Buy me a grandstand ticket, too, would you? Don't want to stint ourselves. And one for Trace, you'll like her, she's great fun. Tracy, stop it. See you then, looking forward to it. I feel lucky today!'

Jackson put the phone down and frowned as he realised a little late that the racecourse setting might not be ideal for lecturing Arthur on prudence. He picked up the phone again to tell Sarah but almost immediately put it down, because, he noted with some irritation, he was feeling guilty. For one afternoon when he hadn't much on anyway. By lunchtime, he had whizzed off a few emails not designed to provoke an immediate response and was feeling more excited than he had for some time.

On his way out, inevitably, he bumped in to Simon Jones. 'Hallo, Jackson. Off anywhere nice? I'm having a working lunch at Berlusconi's with the other trustees of this cancer charity I'm involved with.' How did Jones do it? In one sentence, he had made Jackson feel not only guilty about his lack of voluntary activities as well as his buckshee horsefest but also envious since no one had ever asked him to be the trustee of anything except a will, or a trust. 'No, just popping out for a sandwich,' he lied. 'Then a couple of clients to see this afternoon.' 'Don't work too hard,' said Jones over his shoulder. It wasn't Jones's unerring ability to find a weak spot that was so infuriating, Jackson decided, more that he had no idea he was doing it.

But it was one of those crisp days in early Spring when people are beginning to find their smiles again in the returning sun, and he'd cheered up considerably by the time he arrived at the small, friendly course and picked up on the happy buzz of money to be made before it's lost. Jackson stumped up for three grandstand tickets and made his way to the rails where the bookies were pitched. There was no difficulty spotting Arthur and Tracy. Arthur was wearing a brown trilby and an overcoat of a check vibrant enough to satisfy even the late Frank Harris, writer, rogue and friend of Oscar Wilde, whose bright tweedy racing attire provoked from Edward VII: 'Mornin' Harris. Goin' rattin?' But this was as naught to Tracy, who was dressed for an occasion several degrees higher in both status and temperature, strikingly blonde locks arranged beneath a splendidly trembling fascinator setting off the large amount of decking-tinted skin which her black frock was failing to contain. 'Mr Percival, very good to see you,' said Jackson, 'And you must be Tracy.'

'How did you guess?' said Tracy with the laugh Mark had so well described.

'Call me Arthur,' said Arthur. 'More friendly. That's right, isn't it, Jim?'

'That's right, Arthur,' replied Gentleman Jim, a riot of camel and black velvet detail, without appearing to move his lips. 'You'll be having a bet, Jackson,' said Arthur, gesturing expansively at the runners and odds Jim was displaying in finest dot matrix for the two o'clock race. Jackson was one of those occasional punters who preferred to rely on a resonant name rather than anything as temporary as form or misleading as breeding.

'Badger's Cough,' he said. '£2.50 each way'.

'Blimey,' said Jim, again without moving his lips or removing his stare from the middle distance. 'I shall have to start some serious laying off. What about you, Arthur?'

'Interesting choice,' said Arthur. 'But a touch on the safe side for me. I think I'll go a monkey to win on Final Fling.'

'Hmm, 20-1, attractive odds,' said Jackson. 'How much is a monkey?'

'Five hundred quid,' said Arthur, producing a fat roll of notes. 'No point in mucking about.'

Jackson began to feel a bit dizzy. 'Besides, Jackson,' he said with a wink that was not only telegraphed but emailed and posted on social media as well, 'That mug son of mine will pay up if it goes tits up, sentimental little sod. You were always more fun, Jackson, although it's strictly relative. How's that boring little dentist you got hitched up with?'

'C'mon, Artie,' said Tracy, 'My arms are beginning to fade. Champagne Bar, now!' Jackson mentioned something about there not being much time before the race, but the remarkable couple were already out of earshot, going at a pace that wouldn't have disgraced Aintree, soft going, first time round.

When he got to the bar, the check and the fascinator were at the other end, watching as a bottle of *Veuve Cliquot* was opened, discharged into three glasses and then reverently placed in an ice bucket. 'Bottoms up!' shouted Arthur. If this was a film, thought Jackson, Arthur would now give Tracy a jaunty slap on the bottom, which was of course exactly what he did. 'Ooh, cheeky!' giggled Tracy at a volume that invited attention, not to say alarm, from even those nearby listeners who were not of a nervous disposition.

Jackson, uneasily aware of attention, took a sip of the champagne when he really should have remembered that no one has ever had one glass of the icy tantaliser, not even conveyancing solicitors; not on a Spring afternoon. Arthur was leering at him in a rather disturbing way while the hand not occupied with champagne wandered around Tracy. Jackson took another sip of his and tried some light upbraiding: 'I thought you said you needed subbing.'

'Ah, yes, but that was before Methuselah's Dad came in at 33-1 in the 12.30.'

Jackson found himself, as lawyers so often do, in some difficulty. As he had already acknowledged to himself, the racecourse was only the ideal setting for a spendthrift to recognise the error of his ways if he was losing, which Arthur emphatically wasn't. It was also difficult to compete with Tracy and the champagne for Arthur's attention. Jackson took instructions from himself and decided to wait until after the next race, or the first race which Arthur lost. Meanwhile, he concentrated on his second glass, and then his third, which he had to knock back sooner than he would have liked as they were now off to the Grandstand, Arthur and Tracy setting a smart pace. Jackson fussed along behind, noting with enjoyment the slight giddiness provided by the iced bubbles and the excitement of the occasion.

His tickets proved to be rather good, if a little way up the grandstand. But the sharp raking of the seats gave a fine view as the runners and riders readied for the 2pm race, the Rob Beale Septic Tank Emptying and Temporary Toilets Handicap Hurdle. There was the usual expectant show as the seal-sleek horses and their splashily silked jockeys cantered past to the start, then the lull between sight and PA system as the race began. The commentator was unimpressed with both Badger's Cough and Final Fling, mentioning them from time to time as an afterthought while he concentrated too much for Jackson's taste on the flashy favourite, Dick the Dancer. Still, after the first circuit, both Badger's Cough and Final Fling were still jumping, if not doing anything like well enough to escape the obvious disdain of the commentator, who clearly had next year's school fees riding on Dick the Dancer. Arthur, now smoking a large cigar, was employing language of encouragement that would have shocked Eliza Doolittle; Tracy was demanding regular updates on Final Fling's progress while otherwise engaged head down with her mobile.

Three fences out, though, even Mr Snooty had to notice that both Badger's Cough and Final Fling were moving up the field. Now the Grandstand had a view: Dick the Dancer appeared to be galloping on the spot as the two unfancied horses swept up and by, Badger's Cough ahead by a couple of lengths after a terrific jump at the second last. Jackson was now enjoying that excitement which is racing's greatest gift, the exhilarating contrast with the waiting and the not quite being able to see what's going on. 'Come on, Badger's Cough, come on!' he shouted, on his feet. Some of his more staid clients would have been rather shocked if they could have heard him, but there was no danger of that, as Tracy had hit top volume and even Arthur was drowned out, reduced to making what looked like goldfish mouth movements in the din.

Came the last, and Badger's Cough jumped in the lead, but was badly tiring; Dick the Dancer was coming back, and overtook him six lengths out. Now, though, Final Fling, more than likely fearing and certainly hearing Tracy, found some reserves of speed and strength and just held off Dick the Dancer to take it by a nose at the post. Badger's Cough was third. Jackson congratulated himself on the each-way bet: that would be about £20 by his calculation; and this was only the first race. He was about to exit his row to get his winnings when Arthur and Tracy, both whooping with the joy of luck, squeezed past at pace and were out in front of him, hotfoot for Gentleman Jim. Caught up in the excitement of it all, Jackson hurried after them onto the steps.

As he later told the coroner, on his way down he was nudged forward by the press of spectators following him out of the grandstand; as he struggled to maintain balance one of his flailing arms caught Mrs Siren [aka Tracy], who was just in front of him. They became entangled. Mr Percival, hearing Mrs Siren's cry of alarm, turned as he was hurrying down the steps, lost his footing and fell headlong. His head had crashed into the concrete, and he lost consciousness, never to regain it. His last words were 'What A Lark, dead cert, 3.30'. (Jackson saw no point in mentioning his three glasses of champagne; or that Tracy had rushed to her fallen lover, prised the winning slip from his hand and made off immediately for Gentleman Jim, shouting over her shoulder, 'It's what he would have wanted'.)

No, said Jackson, in common with the coroner's officer, he had been unable to determine Mrs Siren's current whereabouts; he could only conclude that she had taken herself off to try to come to terms with her grief, and it was taking some time. After some deliberation, the inquest jury returned a verdict of accidental death. The coroner recommended consideration be given henceforth to obligatory high-visibility jackets for all grandstand patrons, and added some pointed remarks about gambling, greed and self-control that earned him a front page report in the local newspaper under the headline, 'Coroner Nags Punters After Death Plunge'. What A Lark came in last.

TRACY HADN'T turned up to Arthur's funeral, either. There weren't many mourners, in any case. A few old respectable friends; some others who were quite clearly neither quickly faded away when Mark made it clear that they were not going to be invited back. Mark's ex-wife, Maggie, and his ex-gardener, Bernard, did not attend. Their twins, Hilly and Tilly, both in the city, spent most of the time looking at their phones and left early. Jackson thought Gentleman Jim might have made the effort. Mark himself was looking better than when he had met Jackson and Sarah at the hospital after hurrying up from London on the day of his poor father's abrupt departure. They had gone on to Arthur's house, where some suddenly poignant reminders of the the old man and his latter life style lay littered about: unopened bills, casino chips, race cards, a packet of condoms next to one of Viagra, both opened, a bottle of that scent which comes with a powerboat, and a scarf of a particularly violent hue draped over the sofa.

Mark had listened intently while Jackson told him of the disaster at the racecourse and the grim aftermath of ambulance, hospital and dead-on-arrival. When he'd finished, Mark had been silent for a few seconds, staring in front of him; then he looked directly at Jackson and said: 'I see, I see. Thank you, Jackson, thank you. I knew you were a good friend. I knew I could rely on you. Good friend, Jackson. I'm a bit upset, even though he was a terrible old sod, but thank you.'

'I'm so sorry, Mark,' said Jackson.

'You don't want to stay here,' said Sarah. 'Come home and stay with us.'

They went back and sat around in that lost and slightly aimless way that the just-dead leave behind for the living. Sarah chatted away in the general and familiar manner of the dentist, not expecting an answer because most of the people she usually spoke to couldn't, what with the anaesthetic and the little sucking thing. Both Mark and Jackson were grateful for her presence, as it allowed them to move around Arthur's death with regret and reminiscence, in the English way: indirect, allusive, more anxious not to intrude than to understand, and most anxious not to embarrass anyone, particularly themselves. And so it was that they successfully concealed Jackson's guilt about the champagne and Mark's conviction that his friend had murdered his father.

OF COURSE IT had all been a terrible shock, but Mark, mulling away afterwards, hadn't found it difficult to believe that his friend had acted upon their fatal conversation. Despite all his conventionalities, Jackson had always had a rogue streak, a tendency to unpredictable aberration: the contrast was why Mark relished him. He still remembered vividly the reception in their student days where they'd found themselves in conversation with the then Master of their college. This rare event was becoming ever more awkward and faltering until Jackson suddenly announced, 'Tickle your arse with a feather'. The Master, not trusting his ears, asked Jackson what he'd said. 'Particularly nasty weather,' responded Jackson, holding his senior's gaze for a telling second longer than anyone sensible might.

So Mark was quite prepared to believe that when the chance offered itself, Jackson was ready to take it. Besides, an uncertainty about whether people liked him kept Mark on the look-out for significant gestures of proof, and they didn't come much more significant than this. Good old Jackson! Now it was up to him to keep his side of the agreement. There might be considerable difficulties in hastening his chum's mum's final curtain: she was, after all, in a locked unit with 24-hour care; but, for heaven's sake, he was a crime writer: this sort of thing should be meat and drink to him. So what was it to be? The bogus doctor, as in *Lemon Drizzled*? The hypnotised nurse of *The Battered Berg*? The blackmailed hospital chaplain in *The Sign of the Croissant*? And how to do it? Not as in *Garrotte Cake*, obviously: this called for the gentlest possible dispatch. Poison was too tricky and unpredictable. It would have to be the old pillow farewell, tricky and lengthy with the able-bodied, but a piece of cake with someone as old and infirm as Jilly. Piece of cake: this bloody baking got everywhere, Mark noted to himself, not without satisfaction.

Mark was reasonably familiar with the ways of nursing homes thanks to his late mother-in-law, even if her response to his visits with his ex-wife had always been the same: 'What's that bastard doing here, the bastard?'. He was familiar with the unchallenged occasional visits by less dutiful or more distant relations; and, most importantly, the sensibly trusting way in which carers would confide the door entry code after a couple of visits. The important thing to do was to establish a pattern, a familiarity, a commonplace that would avoid suspicion. He would have to start visiting some time before the deed and continue some time after. He couldn't visit a dead person, so the obvious answer was to begin visiting another resident, clock the routines and whereabouts of Jilly, do the deed, and then gradually wind down his visits to the MacGuffin patient (resisting the temptation to hurry things along, fatally or otherwise).

Mark liked to get his plots fully worked out in advance, so he thought carefully about possible flaws. He could avoid bumping into Jackson at the home by never being there on a Saturday and always checking the visitors' book while pretending to sign in. He hadn't quite decided how to guard against being recognised by a representative of the home at Jilly's funeral; currently it was between wearing a false beard or pleading a clash with an award ceremony for one of his books somewhere in eastern Europe. There was also the possibility of a relation arriving to visit the MacGuffin while he was there; morning visits would be best, with a story about being a voluntary visitor if one did arrive. Mark was quite excited; talk of the Booker with Jackson might have been a bit ambitious, he just about conceded to himself, but, suitably and discreetly adapted, this might just get him a Silver Dagger.

The first visit went reasonably well; or, as he looked back that night, over a stiff drink, as well as could be expected. He'd driven up quite early one Monday, and parked away from Autumn Leaves. He hadn't had to wait long before someone came out of the code-protected front door, allowing him to stop pretending to enter a code and go in with a rueful smile through the false beard (which, of course, he hadn't been able to resist, and was rather pleased with). A study of the visitors' book, pen poised against interruption, showed a pleasing regularity to visits, including Jackson's squiggle every Saturday morning. Mark was looking for someone who visited very regularly but less frequently. Millie looked good: another squiggle, every two or three weeks, always a Sunday afternoon. Mark asked the way to the EMI from a passing carer-in-a-hurry, made his way up the stairs, pressed the door-release switch and walked inside.

He was in a corridor, regulation dado rail with pink below and anonymous pink-based floral wallpaper above. The kitchen led off it to one side, with a lift on the other. A carer was in the kitchen; Mark, over-deferential in the manner of a middle class now unused to servants, asked for Millie. The carer showed no surprise and led the way to the end of the corridor and a lounge, again pinked, with high armchairs in another shade of pink. The television was blaring, daytime television, featuring someone called Willow and a discussion as to whether she should have stabbed her errant partner with a fork. 'Millie, here's a visitor for you,' said the carer, whose name was Sandi, brightly. Millie, a wizened woman, wasn't watching Willow, who was now weeping. Nor were any of the other occupants in the room, all women, in various degrees of stupor. Mark tried to spot Jilly, but it had been some years since he'd last seen her, and dementia does do something for a person.

Millie was in her eighties, Mark estimated, and didn't look like she had long left. 'Hello, auntie,' said Mark. Millie showed no sign of noticing him. He pulled up a smaller chair next to her. Sandi bustled off, no doubt to continue preparing, or rather heating up, what passed for lunch in these places. Millie still showed no sign of noticing him. 'It's Bernard, auntie. How are you?' Millie continued to stare expressionlessly in front of her while Mark prattled on in his guise as Bernard, a very dull gardener living on a houseboat with his wife, Maggie, a silly woman who was continually having the most awful bad luck. "You remember Maggie, Auntie, don't you?", he said, happily aware that here it would have invited more suspicion if Millie could. During his pauses, which Millie refused to fill, Mark looked around, and then remembered this was a dangerous thing to do in these places. A woman with a face of frozen fear was staring at him. He said hello and smiled, but she took no notice, either. Another woman walked in jerkily, muttering to herself and walked out again. Another was singing a song to herself. Mark remembered Jackson's distress and felt some of it himself. He was, after all, a man of sympathy. A murderer, potentially, but a sympathetic one.

'Why are you wearing a false beard?' asked Millie. 'Who are you?'

Mark sensed, though he must have been imagining it, that he had the room's full attention. He felt hot under the beard. 'Very good, auntie,' he said, forcing a laugh and a smile. 'You've just not seen it before. I've only just grown it. Perhaps it needs a trim.'

'Can't stand beards,' said Millie. 'Dad grew a beard once, didn't he? Horrible thing. But it wasn't false like yours.'

A Filipina carer came in. 'Hello, ladies, what are you talking about?' she said, in heavily accented English.

'False beards,' said Millie.

Fortunately, the Filipina's comprehension was not quite up to the concept of bogus hirsutery, so she just laughed and smiled at Mark. A woman who had been sleeping in the corner had now woken and was beginning to get agitated by the noise. The Filipina went over to her, saying, 'Hello, Jilly, how are you? Would you like some tea, my darling?'

Jilly frowned as if she was trying to remember something and then said, 'I'm not your darling'.

The Filipina laughed again, directing it conspiratorially at Mark, who smiled sympathetically back. 'What about you, Jilly? Tea?' Another of the elderly women half-smiled back in a distant way, and the Filipina went off to the kitchen.

Two Jillies! It wasn't like this with fiction. Mark was a little put off his stroke but managed to chat on some more about Maggie's recent accident, when she had slipped in the wet on the houseboat deck and landed on her bottom, one shouldn't laugh, really, quite bruised and finding it difficult to sit down, and it was his fault for not getting round to putting the anti-slip decking strips down, which was slack because they were available from all good DIY stores. He'd managed about 20 minutes when he judged it time to leave. Millie paid no attention. Mark said goodbye to the Filipina and asked her name, which was Grace. He asked her how she thought Millie was: 'She's fine. She gets upset from time to time, but mostly she's fine. She's old,' said Grace, speaking with the loud indiscretion that Mark had long ago decided was part of the shutting-down of sensitivity and imagination that the job demanded: wiping withered bottoms also does something to a person.

Nodding and smiling to the other carers going about their relentlessly ignoble duties in other parts of the unit, Mark found Sandi and asked if she could let him out. Sandi showed the lack of curiosity in visitors that Mark ascribed to the same shutting-down process, and upon which he was relying. She led him to the door where she keyed in the code, straight down the middle, and opened the door, still smiling.

MARK BEGAN visiting weekly, varying his arrivals, but avoiding popular times. Millie started to show some sign of recognising him, without much enthusiasm. 'You're not Simon, are you?' she would say; Mark took Simon to be her son, the indecipherable squiggle in the visiting book. 'No, I'm Bernard, auntie,' he would say.

'Bernard,' she would repeat, unconvinced. 'Beard.' Actually, Mark was now rather more pleased with the beard, which he had now successfully groomed into the full Hoxton, with matching cap and plaid. After a couple of visits, he suggested they should go and sit in Millie's room, where it would be quieter, away from the television, from Irene walking up and down, endlessly, from the eruptions of anger from Rita and the other low-level but incessant moanings and repetitions.

Millie, sitting in the chair next to her bed, seemed to like the change, although she still showed little apparent interest in Mark's tales of Bernard's life and the appalling run of bad and painful luck poor Maggie was still having (most recently injured in another freak accident, involving a pancake). As Millie continued to stare, Mark slipped out to check the names on the other inmates' rooms. He found Jilly Jackson's at the end of the corridor, next to Jilly Duke's. As there seemed to be some bustling and talking going on inside Jilly Jackson's room, Mark withdrew back along the corridor and re-entered Millie's room. After his cheery hello had as usual failed to provoke a response, he got back into the swing of a Bernard and Maggie story. 'Who would have thought you could possibly get seasick on a houseboat? Poor Maggie!' It was at this point that Mark noticed Millie was dead.

Which complicated matters. Not only would an ex-Millie remove his excuse for visiting Autumn Leaves, but he might also get caught up without answers in her farewell arrangements. And clearly moving swiftly back down the hall to attend to Jilly wasn't going to work, either, as two deaths, even of such vintages, on the same day around the same time were almost inevitably bound to provoke suspicion. Mark approached the immobile Millie and bent down to shake her gently on the shoulder and call her name into her right ear. Nothing. Drawing on his professional expertise, he got out his mobile and placed it in front of her mouth: no misting. Millie was gone, definitely.

Rather impressed with his calm, Mark weighed up the options. He didn't like to let his friend down; besides, like most friends, he was competitive. Maybe he could still come up with something; but, in the meantime, this was no place to be found loitering even without intent. He opened the door and went into the corridor, where Jackson and a man he didn't recognise were standing in muted conversation. 'Mark!' said Jackson, his voice strident with surprise and growing alarm, 'What are you doing here?'. 'Why,' said the other man, with matching bafflement, 'have you been visiting my mother?' 'Jackson!' said Mark, mustering all that appeared to be immediately available, 'How are you?'. 'As well as can be expected for someone whose mother's just died,' said Jackson. The other man made to push past him to enter Millie's room. Mark asked himself what Saul Pinewood would do in such challenging circumstances and waited urgently for a reply.

JACKSON, UNDERSTANDABLY, found it difficult to slip back into his routine after Arthur's death. He stopped feeling guilty fairly quickly, convincing himself by repetition that the real culprit was the crowd pushing him from behind, and that, although this took more work, the three glasses of champagne were a minor irrelevance. It was also useful to remember quite how dreadful Arthur had become. Moreover, his memory of the *Strangers on a Train* conversation was not as clear as Mark's; or was not allowed to be: Jackson had developed a mental technique for dealing with the uncomfortable that derived from cricket. Rather than burying it, he imagined himself delicately deflecting it, sending it gliding past him in the direction of fine leg, never to return.

Other things had come up, too. There was the latest question that had arisen *re* the badger or badgers: could you shoot one in self-defence? In a startling example of life imitating Jackson's imagination, his opposite number was now demanding that Jackson's client should also insure his client against a badger using the sett that travelled under and into the next door garden to enter the said garden and attempt to attack the next door neighbour, leaving the said neighbour with no option but to shoot the badger, thus laying himself open to the possibility of legal action under the badger protection legislation, which was unclear on the specific point, cull or no cull. Jackson's client was showing worrying signs of digging his heels in on this, which meant Jackson was going to have to do quite some research on badger attacks, rarity of. And what test would be applied to the neighbour's state of mind when he shot the putative badger: how scared would he have to be, and how justified did that fear have to be? There was also the nuclear option: a full-scale excavation to clarify the exact layout of the sett and determine whether it had incontrovertibly originated in Jackson's client's garden. But this was the last thing he wanted as it would delay the sale.

Weighty matters. And Sarah was leaving him. The distance, the eagerness for him to go away had become clear: a *coup de foudre* during a replacement crown procedure. An Australian visiting relatives who wanted to take her back to the crocodile farm in Queensland. Jackson was bothered that he wasn't more bothered, but suspected that he was in denial and would only come out of it when she was 10,000 miles away wrangling reptiles. The children seemed relieved if not especially concerned. And Sarah did seem very happy, when he saw her, although he had yet to be introduced to Kerry, as the Australian seemed to be called. Nor was he entirely sure what he had to offer in competition: more of the same didn't quite cut it, and he couldn't think of the equivalent of a crocodile farm in their area; Farmer Bob's Petting Zoo didn't have quite the same feel.

Simon Jones was being his usual irritating self, and had started wandering into Jackson's office and wondering aloud in his usual irritating way about how they, or specifically, Jackson, could bring in some more work to the practice, what about all his posh Oxford connections, get out more, conferences, workshops, local chambers, Rotary, can't wait for them to come to us any more, you know, not in this climate, otherwise might be looking at a leaner practice, hate to do it, but it might have to happen, so sorry to hear about Sarah, been to Australia, hadn't liked it, what could she possibly see in a koala keeper?

Jackson thought he detected some sympathy in this last bit but quickly dismissed the idea as it was far too inconvenient and at odds with the character he had constructed for Jones. Besides it was embarrassing. He might be careless of being a cuckold, but society did make certain demands. So he got up from his desk quickly, saying he had to go to see his mother. This was true. The home had been on; one of the carers was worried about Jilly. It had happened before, when Jackson had been brought sharply up against the dementia dilemma, hoping and not hoping that she would pull through. Jones asked which home Jilly was in. 'Really?', he said, then said it again. 'Really? That's amazing. My mum's there, too. Which one's yours?' Jackson was taken aback, and further irritated. No escape from Jones, anywhere. 'Jilly,' he said. 'Which one's yours?'

'Millie,' said Jones.

'Jilly's your mum?' said Jones. 'Jilly Jackson. Of course. I've seen her name on the door of her room now I think of it and never put two and two together.'

'Ditto,' muttered Jackson. 'Anyway, I'd better get up there.'

'Let me take you,' said Jones. 'It'll be the usual false alarm. We can continue our little brainstorming session and I can pop in and see Mummy, she can pay as much attention as usual, and I won't have to go this Sunday. Result all round. Come on.'

Jackson, trapped, followed Jones to the car park. 'New dent?' said Jones, pointing to Jackson's latest encounter with his gatepost. Jackson grunted and got into Jones's Mercedes. To forestall any more practice talk, he started a note-swap over their mothers. He'd placed Millie now, one of the ghosts, like Jilly. 'We put her in about four months ago. Poor dear was going down, couldn't look after herself any longer. We'd liked to have had her live with us, obviously, but we're moving house and Caroline thought the disruption would do her no good and she didn't see how she could make it work, configuration-wise.'

'I didn't know you were moving,' said Jackson. 'I hope the new house doesn't have electric gates.'

'Ha, very good, forgotten about that. Still don't understand why you didn't slip the old Saab into reverse when you saw them coming at you.'

'So where's the new place?'

Jones, uncharacteristically, hesitated. 'Ah, yes. Sett Hill. Actually, you know the place. Brockside?'

'Brockside! That's one of mine!'

'Yes, I know,' said Jones, now definitely embarrassed. 'I'm afraid we played a bit of an airshot there. Rather assumed the firm would be doing the conveyancing, then found the vendors had already instructed you.'

'But the purchaser is somebody else. It's, oh, right, it's Miss Caroline Prydecombe.'

'The same.'

'She's very fussy, isn't she? Or is that you?'

Another pause. Jackson was now rather enjoying himself. 'No, that's Caroline.'

'You seem very bothered about the badgers.'

'Yes. Perhaps we shouldn't talk about it. Chinese walls and whatnot. Anyway, as you'll know, there isn't really any room for Mummy'.

'It's got eight bedrooms.'

'We do a lot of entertaining.'

They turned into Autumn Leaves, climbed out of the Mercedes as elegantly as middle-aged solicitors could, and walked towards the door, where a blonde woman in a faux-leopard print coat reaching down to high boots was angrily punching and swearing at the door code panel. 'Tracy!' said Jackson. Tracy looked at Jackson blankly. 'Can you work this bloody thing? It's changed since I was last here, and that was only a bloody year ago.'

'Yes, they had to change it after a bad run on pizza deliveries. Tracy, it's Philip Jackson, remember, the racecourse and Arthur?'

'Remember? How could I forget? I gave that old bugger some of the best minutes of my life and then he pisses off permanento just when he was finally going to change his will like he'd always promised. Not a good way to go, though, was it, before he'd collected. I've got the money, well, spent it, to be honest, couldn't see the point of Gentleman Jim keeping it. Anyway, can't stand around here, nice as it is to see you again, Jackson, and your friend, I'm sure. I've got to go and see the old bat to see if she's remembered where she put her savings.'

'Your mum's here?'

'Jilly Duke. Last of the sodding survivors. No brains left but nobody's told the rest of her. Pity she can't be bumped off. Save everybody a lot of trouble. I'd do it, I would. Just need to find about about the savings first. Sorry to be blunt, but you know me, Jack, I speak my mind, I'm straight. Cost me a couple of marriages, to a couple of bastards. You both married?'

Tracy was flirting with Jones, who seemed rather receptive, which did not surprise Jackson, as he knew Caroline. They made the familiar way up to the EMI unit. Sandi met them. "My, what a lot of visitors today!" she said, not quite as brightly as usual. "They're all in their rooms. The doctor's with your mother," she said to Jackson. 'Is she all right?' he asked.

'Yes, love,' said Sandi, with slightly less than her usual cheery conviction.

'She means there's no point bringing her a pot plant,' said Tracy.

Jackson went to his mother, leaving Jones and Tracy, who seemed in no hurry to visit theirs, in conversation. 'Well, actually, I'm his boss,' Jones was saying. 'Have you been in the new Mercedes?'

Jilly was dead, though most of her had gone before much earlier. Jackson searched for something to tell himself that wasn't a cliché and couldn't. He went back into the corridor, lost for a moment, shocked by the life departed. Tracy had gone into to see her mother. Jones was still there, looking for an excuse to shorten the time he would spend with his. Irene was walking up and down and out and back, muttering, followed by May, whose rising scream seemed louder and more questioning today. Tracy's voice was getting louder and louder; evidently her mother had not yet been able to remember the whereabouts of the savings. Jackson gave his sad news to Jones, who was once more inconveniently sympathetic. Then Millie's door opened, and out came Mark, wearing his false beard.

'Mark!' said Jackson, his voice strident with surprise and growing alarm, 'What are you doing here?'.

'Why,' said Jones, with matching bafflement, 'have you been visiting my mother?'

'Jackson!' said Mark, after a pause, 'How are you?'.

'As well as can be expected for someone whose mother's died,' said Jackson.

Jones made to push past Mark to enter Millie's room. 'Bloody hell, it's stuffy Mark, in a beard!' said Tracy, who had just come into the corridor. There was what could with complete accuracy be described as an awkward silence before Mark said, 'Got to dash, I've just remembered I left something in the oven'.

IT'S FAIR to say that Mark didn't emerge too well from this particular inquest. There were, noted the coroner, certain glaring inconsistencies in his account. It was, he allowed, conceivably credible that he could have been visiting the deceased, Mrs Millie Jones, under the misapprehension that she was Mrs Jilly Jackson, the mother of a friend, for the purposes of research in furtherance of a novel he was writing. But there had not been a satisfactory explanation for the false identity – and the false beard – that he had assumed to so do. Mr Percival had doubtless gained some *éclat* in the world of the whodunnit – and indeed, added the coroner, he himself had enjoyed several of Saul Pinewood's outings, including *The Sign of the Croissant* – but he surely had no need, as he claimed, to disguise himself against unwanted recognition and unwelcome attention, particularly in a dementia unit.

Nevertheless, in the complete absence of any evidence that Mrs Jones's demise had been anything other than the result of natural causes, he had no option but to record such a verdict. He also wanted to put on record his sympathy for Mr Jones, a longstanding friend of the court; and to warn writers, no matter how successful, against taking their research too far. This time, the headline read, 'Coroner's Bad Review For Best Seller'.

The publicity did Mark's sales no harm at all. They received a further boost when Maggie fell off the houseboat and drowned. Fortunately he was at the Hay Literary Festival at the time giving his talk, *'Gas Mark Zero: Death and the Baker'*. The coroner upbraided Bernard Charnock for not fitting anti-slip strips. Jackson's friendship with Mark, like his relationship with Simon Jones, never recovered. Jackson gave up the law and is now a croupier in Reno. Professor Roby wasn't surprised. Sarah went to Queensland with Kerry, who was, Jackson discovered when he finally met her, a woman. Tracy had quite a few rides in the Mercedes. The badgers doubled back and are now fairly near the foundations of Brockside.

'To lose one parent may be regarded as a misfortune; to lose both looks like carelessness.' Oscar Wilde, The Importance of Being Earnest.

THE QUIET CARRIAGE +++

Scene One...

(Noises of a train in transit, the Quiet Carriage.)

MARTIN: *(Via the PA system) This is MARTIN, your executive client services executive, speaking. I'd like to welcome on board those clients who joined us at Kirby Muxloe. I'm sure we're all very pleased to see you, aren't we, clients who joined earlier? Even the clients in the Quiet Carriage, although they might not be showing it. Our next station stop is Desford, known in polite circles of course as Desmondford. Boom, boom, as the engine said to the buffers. I thank you, over and out, roger.*

HENRY: *(Sighs heavily.)* A comedian. That's all we need.

KATE: Excuse me, is this seat taken?

HENRY: *(Sighs heavily, again.)* No, please.

(There's the sound of belongings being moved, with more sighs.)

KATE: *(Unimpressed with her welcome.)* I'm terribly sorry to disturb you, but I'm afraid there's nowhere else to sit.

HENRY: *(Grunts.)*

(Sounds of KATE making herself comfortable, including the raising and lowering of the tray in front of her, and the shuffling of papers etc.)

KATE: Sorry, is this Topkidz Tornado bubblegum wrapper yours? It was on the tray.

HENRY: No, it is not. Now if you'll excuse me, I'd like to get on with my book.

KATE: I've read it. She throws herself under a train.

HENRY: Thanks very much. Sorry to disappoint you, but I've read it before.

KATE: Well done. Why people read books again when there's an almost infinite supply of ones they haven't is beyond me. Fear, narrowness, lack of imagination, something like that I suppose.

HENRY: Indeed. Probably the sort of person who listens to a piece of music again or looks at a fine painting again. Probably also the sort of person who doesn't necessarily welcome the sudden proximity of another person marshalling forces and an elbow on the disputed frontier of his personal space.

KATE: Terrible, indeed. And the sort of person who misses out on such a lot, including a rather good story I know about Dan Quayle and your book which I don't often get the chance to tell since he stopped being American vice president.

HENRY: Dan Quayle? The one who couldn't spell potato properly all those years ago? I'm supposed to care? Please let me read my book.

KATE: He asked a reporter following him on the campaign trail what was the book she was reading. When she told him it was *Anna Karenina*, he furrowed his brow, closed his eyes, opened them again, and said, 'Russian, right?'

HENRY: (*Laughs in spite of himself.*) Do you always speak to strangers on a train?

KATE: Only when they've annoyed me.

(*A pause. More train noises.*)

MARTIN: *Hello, ladies and gentlemen, esteemed clients, it is I, Martin, your executive client service executive, again. Just to remind you that your buffet car is now open for our yummy hot and cold snacks and beverages. Your buffet car is situated between the Special Gold VIP Standard Class and the Special Special Gold VIP Standard Class carriages, so that all our clients can mingle to their mutual satisfaction and see how the other half lives. And worry not, Specials, I am able to upgrade you to Special Special for a very reasonable supplement providing you shop at Waitrose and don't live in the North of England. Another of my little jokes there! Bye for now. And always remember that I am truly dedicated to being at your service because, wait for it, my job is on the line!*

KATE: God.

HENRY: Everybody thinks they can be a comedian these days. Not surprising, really, when you see the sort of smug creatures who smile proudly at their own tired and obvious observations on these endless quiz shows. Where's Chic Murray when you need him?

KATE: Blimey, it must be fun being you. I suppose you'd better tell me. Who's Chic Murray?

HENRY: Ah, now you're talking. Chic Murray. Scots comic, really funny. When the genteel Edinburgh landlady brought him a very small portion of honey, he looked at it and said, 'I see you keep a bee'. Chic Murray. You should Google him.

KATE: I'm surprised you've heard of Google. You'll be telling me you're on Youtube next, when you're not Instagramming.

HENRY: Youtube's great, isn't it? You should try Mr Pastry on it, comedy gold. Mr Pastry. He dressed up as an old bloke and fell over a lot, marvellous. I love Google, too. It arrived just as my memory was failing. Seamless transition, although I have to pass on the information pretty quickly before it goes again. Actually, I'm thinking of having that thing on Wiki as my epitaph. 'Citation Needed,' it will say on my gravestone. A friend of mine is pretty keen on 'He died requiring snookers' for his. Snooker. It used to be very popular on the telly.

KATE: Come on, I'm not that young. I can even remember how viewers complained when the BBC interrupted a fairly tense game to bring live coverage of the SAS storming the Iranian Embassy.

HENRY: God, yes. Cliff 'The Grinder' Thorburn against Alex 'The Hurricane' Higgins, great match, gripping contrast in styles.

KATE: I thought you said your memory was failing.

HENRY: Well, yes, for the important things. I can't remember who won, for example.

KATE: The SAS.

HENRY: That's very good. I can almost forgive you for telling me the end of *Anna Karenina*.

KATE: You said you'd read it before.

HENRY: You didn't know that.

KATE: You were bloody rude.

HENRY: Sorry. Bit grumpy on trains. Bit grumpy all the time, to be honest. Too many years spent fruitlessly trying to instil a love of learning into the closed and crazed mind of the adolescent, the little swine. I'm Henry, by the way.

KATE: Well, perhaps I was a bit grumpy as well. Too many years spent fruitlessly trying to instil a semblance of respect into men, the little swine. I'm Kate.

HENRY: They are terribly cramped, these seats, though, aren't they?

KATE: Why aren't you in the Special Special Gold VIP Standard Class? There's another 14 centimetres in there.

HENRY: How on earth do you know that?

KATE: Google isn't exclusive, you know. They allow women on as well. And I wasn't always the Special Gold VIP Standard Class person you see before you. Once I was a Special Special Gold VIP Standard Class person.

HENRY: What happened? Were you banned for not wearing black?

KATE: I was found not to be in possession of a screen and a suitably glazed expression.

HENRY: By Martin, our executive client services executive?

(The sound of the train slowing and stopping with a bit of a jerk.)

MARTIN: *Hello clients. An unscheduled stop, I'm afraid. Let me see what's going on. I'll be back to you as soon as I've had a word with Dave, our director of propulsion – that's train driver to you, clients! Meanwhile, this is Adlestrop. Adlestrop. I know it looks very tempting on this fine late June afternoon, but please don't alight as I'm sure we will resume our forward trajectory momentarily.*

Scene Two…

(*Silence, bar the song of a blackbird.*)

HENRY: Adlestrop. I know the name, but can't quite remember why. Very quiet and still, isn't it?

KATE: Yes, lovely willows and meadowsweet. *(The blackbird, again.)* Was that a blackbird?

HENRY: No, I think you'll find that was a Crested Grebe, or possibly a Great Knot.

KATE: A great knot what?

HENRY: What? No, not not, knot. With a k. Very rare.

KATE: I'm pretty sure it's a blackbird *(The blackbird, again)*.

HENRY: What a quintessential English countryside scene! Peaceful, serene, timeless.

KATE: The supermarket trolley is a nice touch.

HENRY: A lot of the old ticket halls are pizza franchises now, aren't they?

KATE: Look, that must be Dave, the director of propulsion, stretching his legs. He seems a bit shifty, doesn't he?

HENRY: Not as shifty as the woman approaching him.

KATE: I see what you mean. It's the way she keeps looking to the left and then to the right and then behind her.

HENRY: And pausing to hide behind every second pillar.

KATE: She's giving him something! Some sort of package.

HENRY: Very dodgy. Probably a good idea to take off your hi visibility jacket if you're going to do that, I should have said. Does rather catch the eye.

(*Sound of the train starting.*)

MARTIN: *Well, clients, apologies for that slight delay, which, Dave tells me, was caused by a minor system failure which totally incapacitated our forward motion, leaving us completely at the mercy of any following trains whose directors of propulsion weren't paying attention. Anyway, he's switched it off and switched it back on again and everything now seems fine. As you can probably tell, Dave is very anxious to make up for lost time, so I'd advise you to lean right back, clutch the arm rests very tightly and brace your knees hard against the seat in front of you.*

KATE: Hmm. This is all very suspicious, isn't it?

HENRY: No, not really. A little unusual, perhaps. Good thing that bag which fell from the luggage rack and bounced off the old lady was a light one, though. Game old bird, isn't she?

KATE: For a teacher, you're not very pro-active, are you, Henry?

HENRY: What a dreadful word. Next you'll be telling me I've got issues around issues that I should be addressing if I want to achieve closure any time soon.

KATE: Thank you, Mr Chips. I think you're right, you have been teaching for too long. You are still teaching, I take it?

HENRY: Sort of.

KATE: Sort of?

HENRY: I'm a driving instructor.

KATE: You're a driving instructor?

HENRY: Yes, I gave up academic teaching. The little swine got to me. The indifference, indolence, insolence and the insistent, insidious threat of worse. At least with this you can see where their hands are.

KATE: But if you're a driving instructor, why are you on a train?

HENRY: Have you seen the roads? Jams, appalling manners, speeding, crashes, rage, repeated failure to check rear view mirrors before indicating? You won't get me out there unless it's absolutely necessary.

KATE: It doesn't sound as if it's quite the ideal job for you.

HENRY: No, but you have to make compromises, don't you? You can't always get what you want, as Sir Mick used to put it. I'd rather have two seats on here, for example.

KATE: Thanks a lot.

(Silence: nothing but the sound of the rattling train.)

MARTIN: *Hello, speedsters! You'll be delighted to know that Dave has made up the delay and that we will shortly be arriving on time at our next train-station-on-a-railway-line-momentary-stop-before-starting-again, Milford Junction.*

HENRY: What was that?

MARTIN: *Milford Junction. Milford Junction, our next train-station-on-a-railway-line-momentary-stop-before-starting-again. Change here for Titfield, Tumby Woodside and Buggleskelly. Clients taking the train from Platform Three are advised to put it back again.*

HENRY: Heaven preserve us.

(Sound of train stopping, passengers moving, internal and external carriage doors opening and closing.)

HENRY: You are talking to me, aren't you? That bit about the seats was a joke that went a touch wrong. I do tend to do that, sorry.

KATE: Accepted. You're a man, Henry. Intimacy terrifies you. I understand.

HENRY: Now that's a bit stiff, as the actress said to the bishop.

KATE: Precisely.

(Sound of muffled shouts from the platform.)

HENRY: What on earth is going on now?

KATE: I can't see. Oh, wait a moment. It's Dave. He's hurled his hi-vis to the ground and is stamping on it. And now he's storming off, followed by three men who are still wearing theirs.

HENRY: Goodness me, what a trip this is turning into!

Scene Three…

(Sounds of the train getting underway)

MARTIN: *Hello, there. I should like to welcome all clients who joined us at Milford Junction. I'm sure we're all very pleased to see you, aren't we, clients who joined earlier? Even the clients in the Quiet Carriage, although they might not be showing it. We have been having an eventful trip, though, haven't we? I expect some of you noticed a bit of a kerfuffle on the platform back there at Milford Junction. It involved our former Director of Propulsion, Dave, and his refusal to accept the company regulation that forbids Directors of Propulsion from ingesting while propelling. His wife was detected providing him with a Hawaiian pizza at Adlestrop. Have you ever tried to combine a Hawaiian pizza with any other activity? You certainly won't find our new Director of Propulsion, Jensen, at it.*

HENRY: Quite right, too. Disgusting things. Safety of passengers paramount. But all this talk of food is making me hungry. Would you like one of my fish paste sandwiches?

MARTIN: *Martin again, clients. All this talk of food must be making you hungry. I'd like to recommend once again our buffet car, which is situated between the Special Special VIP Gold Class carriages and the Special VIP Gold Class carriages. Your beautiful client assistant agent today is Helga, who, like all our client assistance agents, is really passionate about her work. I'd also like to remind clients that they are contractually forbidden to consume foodstuffs which they have prepared themselves as we have to protect our other clients and services from the potentially unhygienic conditions under which they might have been produced. So form an orderly rush to our spotless buffet car now. Thank you.*

HENRY: Cheek!

KATE: Oh, dear. Although in one sense, that's a bit of a relief, as I don't like fish paste, and I'd hate to hurt your feelings.

HENRY: Goodness me, I don't know what I'd do without the regular infusion of fish paste. Almost as good as sandwich spread. Don't worry, you can join me in a piece of Battenberg for afters. I'd offer you some of my Dandelion & Burdock, but I've only got one straw.

KATE: You're not married, Henry, are you?

HENRY: Good spot. Never seemed to get round to it, somehow. How did you guess?

KATE: Some sixth sense, and the corduroys.

HENRY: Yes, I suppose it is pretty obvious. Classic case, really. All male school, no sisters, always slightly nervous of women. Anyway, it's a bit overrated, this romantic business, isn't it? What did Kipling say? 'A woman is only a woman, but a good cigar is a smoke'.

MARTIN: *May I remind clients that smoking is not permitted anywhere on this train.*

KATE: Oh, come on, Henry, that's pretty pathetic. You're not that bad looking, even in beige. And you are reading *Anna Karenina.*

HENRY: And I have read it before. I cry when I'm watching *Brief Encounter*, too, but I also cry when the centaurs capture Professor Umbridge in *Harry Potter.*

KATE: Dolores Umbridge? The mean, narrow-minded, vicious villain played so memorably by Imelda Staunton?

HENRY: She's just trying to do a very difficult job with an unruly set of pupils with some really challenging special needs.

KATE: Oh, right, further attempt at humour to deflect intrusive questioning possibly provoking awkward introspection and uncomfortable conclusions.

HENRY: Listen, there's no need to be insulting just because you don't like fishpaste sandwiches. Or to sound like a psychotherapist.

KATE: I am a psychotherapist.

HENRY: Strewth. Freud or Jung?

KATE: You make it sound like a choice between cooking methods. Jung.

HENRY: That's a pity. I know a rather interesting but little known fact about Freud.

KATE: Go ahead, she said, much against her better judgement.

HENRY: He visited Blackpool as a young man, twice, and was much taken with the Tower. Thus the phallic symbolism of the Lancashire Las Vegas has a key but unacknowledged role in the history of psychoanalysis.

KATE: Very good, Henry. Actually, I'm not a psychotherapist. I just said it to unsettle you.

HENRY: Well it worked. All that listening to dreams. God, other people's dreams are dull, aren't they? Even my own bore me. Nothing exciting ever happens. Still, listening to dreams must be better than listening to other people's problems and then repeating them back as questions.

MARTIN: *Hello, again, clients. I'm afraid we've got another problem? You may have noticed that our speed has become somewhat moderated. Jensen, our new director of propulsion tells me that it will be sorted out as soon as the company puts some more money in the meter. Good sense of humour, old Jensen, quite a change from Dave, I can tell you. The truth is that we have encountered an unseasonable profusion of flattened plant structures on the line which is temporarily hindering our destination attainment. In the meantime, might I suggest that you access the view through one of our transparent window facilities? But please don't count the sheep until you have removed any sharp objects from in front of you and placed your trays in the upright position.*

HENRY: I might become a danger to Martin with a sharp object myself shortly. So what about you?

Married? Or are you in a relationship, as it now seems to be called, like protons and neutrons or something you have with your bank manager.

KATE: Don't be so stuffy, Henry. Never mind the state, you're even frightened of the term. No, I'm not in a relationship, but I was married.

HENRY: Sorry to hear that. About the marriage, I mean.

KATE: No need.

HENRY: What happened?

KATE: He ran off with the Latvian cleaner. Their house is absolutely spotless, I understand.

HENRY: That's terrible, I'm sorry.

KATE: It's not so bad. I don't need a cleaner now he's gone.

HENRY: Right, ok. *(pause)* Sorry, didn't mean to pry.

KATE: That's all right. It's actually quite exciting, starting a new life.

HENRY: So what do you do now?

KATE: I'm a governess.

HENRY: A governess? What year are we in?

KATE: Get with the beat, Baggy! Governesses are the new now thing, especially among the West Asian elites.

HENRY: West Asian elites? Oh, I see, Russians!

KATE: A certain element of re-branding is taking place, yes, in a sensible attempt to counter a grossly misconceived image suggestive of unsophisticated consumption financed from somewhat opaque revenue sources.

HENRY: Goodness me, Kate, now you're sounding like a cross between Martin and Robert Peston!

KATE: I thought that would wind you up. You're just jealous that you're overseeing three point turns while I wander round Knightsbridge and Gstaad and places like that.

HENRY: Jealous? Don't be ridiculous. But you do rather conjure an image of timid women with plain looks but hearts of gold bearing a firm moral compass and copping off with brooding and conveniently widowed squires with secrets. Not that you're timid, obviously. Or plain. All right, I am jealous. Where else do you go?

KATE: You're blushing, Henry. Just places.

HENRY: I am not. It's just a bit stuffy in here. Come on, give me more of a flavour.

KATE: Well, to be honest, I don't know. This is my first position. Very nice family. He's a former Captain in the Russian navy now heavily engaged in direct mergers and acquisitions off the coast of Somalia. He's a widower with seven children who all like singing, apparently. It's my job to teach them until they go off to some vastly expensive public school. I start next week and I'm just off to buy a few things.

HENRY: Ha! And what are your qualifications, exactly, for stocking these eager young Caucasian minds?

KATE: A First from Oxford in English and Russian.

HENRY: Ah.

KATE: Where were you?

HENRY: I don't hold with all this intellectual snobbery.

KATE: Right.

MARTIN: *Hello, it is I, Martin your executive client services executive for today once again, but this time with some serious news. I regret to announce that following an unfortunate incident involving Helga and a purchaser of one of our yummy Kentucky-style-classic blueberry muffins, low in calories but high in yumminess, the buffet car will be closed until further notice for reconfiguration involving the remedying of a precipitation of potato crisps and the restoration of scattered relish sachets. Unfortunate, but I could have warned the purchaser that Helga does not warm to untoward comments about her muffins. Our next train-station-on-a-railway-line-momentary-stop-before-starting-again will be Felpersham.*

Scene Four…

(Halted at Felpersham.)

KATE: Oh, dear. That must be the bloke who had the run-in with Helga over there.

HENRY: Which one?

KATE: The one holding the blood-stained handkerchief to his nose.

HENRY: Good grief, I thought that was polkadot. But you're right, I can see some crumbs round his mouth.

KATE: He's lying across two seats now. I'd better go and see if he's all right.

(Sounds of bustle, Kate getting up, going over and returning.)

HENRY: What did he say?

KATE: Well, he's rambling a bit, actually. Seems in shock. But he did say to watch out for Helga's left hook. Apparently she feints with her right first.

(Sounds of train stopping.)

MARTIN: *This is Felpersham. This is Felpersham. Could I advise Special Special Gold VIP Standard Class passengers who are detraining to remember to take their belongings with them and Special Gold passengers to remember not to take anyone else's belongings with them. Joke, joke, from your loveable rascal of an executive etcetera. Thank you for travelling with us today and we look forward to seeing you again providing you're better behaved, don't we, Helga?*

(Sounds of passengers leaving and arriving, doors slamming etc.)

KATE: Do you know, all joking apart, I'm not sure whether this trip is worth it. Drivers making unscheduled stops to take on pizzas, then clattering along at a speed that wouldn't disgrace Thorpe Park, diktats about fish paste usage and now some poor fellow being punched for complaining about a stale muffin.

HENRY: Better keep your voice down, Kate. It's always the bolshy ones they come for first.

KATE: Very funny. They won't be coming for you, then, Henry. You'll just carry on your low-level grumbling in the English way and nothing will get done, nothing will change, as usual.

HENRY: I happen to admire the English way, especially the grumbling and the buggering on in spite of everything. It's what won us the war. There's an excellent story about Ed Murrow, the American journalist, in a cab in London during the Blitz, contemplating the smoking wreckage of another bombed street, and the cabbie saying, 'Do you know, sir, they'll do that once too often.'

KATE: The old guff. The Americans won us the war. And the Russians.

HENRY: Ah, yes, your new employers. You're obviously helping to repay our debt.

KATE: All right, fair point. He has got a beard, but I don't think he's really a pirate. And at least I'm engaging with the real world, not living in some idealised past that allows you a lofty disengagement when you're not doing your, your…

HENRY: Hill starts. All right, you may have something of an argument there. But hill starts are nothing, it's the mini roundabout that's the full-on confrontation with the real dog-eat-dog world.

KATE: How long are we going to wait here exactly, do you think?

HENRY: Absolutely typical. I'm going to be late now.

KATE: Look, there's goes the muffin man. He's still very pale.

HENRY: Bit short with the bloke collecting for the Red Cross, though, wasn't he?

KATE: I wonder who he's on the phone to? Police, I shouldn't be surprised. He's certainly pointing at the train. But why didn't he call ahead from in here?

HENRY: Don't be silly. This is the Quiet Carriage.

KATE: Of course.

HENRY: Do you know Felpersham?

KATE: Looks very quiet. Don't suppose much happens round here. It'd suit you, Henry.

(Sound of doors slamming and train leaving.)

MARTIN: *Hello, good afternoon and welcome to the clients who joined us at Felpersham. A pity the lady with the loud voice and the bicycle just failed to get on board, a gallant effort. Now I'm afraid I have to remind all clients that we do not tolerate aggressive behaviour towards our highly trained and motivated staff, in this instance questioning in a supposedly amusing fashion the year of manufacture of one of our yummy Kentucky-style-classic blueberry muffins. As I mentioned earlier, the beautiful Helga is passionate about her muffins and I make no apology for that. All good points, as the engine said to the track. Over and out.*

KATE: I'm beginning to like that man's tone less and less. It's all about them, not us, the clients, isn't it?

HENRY: Careful, you're starting to sound like me, Kate.

KATE: Lawks, I'll be complaining about the decline in respect next and asking why things just can't have simple knobs and dials like they did in the old days, that was good enough for us. Where are you going, anyway?

HENRY: Oh, just for a day out, that sort of thing.

KATE: Anywhere special?

HENRY: Yes, well, no, you know.

KATE: Henry, you seem a touch embarrassed. Are you off on a date? Are you on a computer date?

HENRY: No, I am not!

KATE: He doth protest too much! You are, aren't you? I hope you've told her about the fish paste and the corduroys.

HENRY: Listen, I am not going on a date!

KATE: Better keep your voice down, Henry. This, I must remind you, as you're so keen on it, is the Quiet Carriage. We wouldn't want you being handed over to Helga for some urgent re-education, would we? So what are you doing?

HENRY: I don't want to tell you. You'll just laugh.

KATE: Well, well. What can it be? You're off to get some new driving gloves. Dandelion and Burdock running low?

HENRY: All right, all right. I'm going to the model railway show at Olympia. It's a hobby of mine. It doesn't dominate my life. I do not wear a train driver's hat while I am pursuing it. You might be surprised by the names of other enthusiasts: Tim Berners Lee. Winston Churchill. Johnny Cash. Herman Goering. Jack Teagarden, the legendary jazz trombonist, used to invite girls up to his room to see his model train.

KATE: Jack "Mr Relaxed" Teagarden? The mesmeric Louis Armstrong sideman?

HENRY: You like jazz?

KATE: Not since Swing was killed off by the siren simplicities of pop music and the complex pretensions of Charlie Parker. Basie's my man.

HENRY: Yes! Would you like to come up and see *my* trains sometime?

MARTIN: *Hello, again, 'tis I, Martin, your executive client service executive. Do you know, we are all on a journey. A journey that, in one sense, has a clear and fixed destination, although we are running approximately 15 minutes late at present, due to the delay caused by that unseasonable profusion of flattened plant structures and a spot of re-coupling carried out by Helga at Felpersham. But I like to think that we are also on another journey, a journey of discovery, discovery of ourselves and others, of our needs and their needs. That's why I'm delighted to announce that the Buffet Car is now open again for the sale of anything that might tickle your fancy in the snack and beverage department, including our now legendary Classic Kentucky-style blueberry muffins. Not legendary in the sense of old, though, I rush to add before there's any more trouble. Now then: what do you call a train eating a blueberry muffin, Clients? A chew-chew train. Keep on snacking, over and out.*

HENRY: You're right, he is getting worse, isn't he?

KATE: Ah, yes, we are all on a journey. My ex-husband was very fond of using that in his sermons. I didn't realise that he was going to stop to take on the Latvian cleaner, though.

HENRY: His sermons? Your husband was a vicar?

KATE: A lay preacher. Although he wasn't much of either.

HENRY: It must have been very hurtful.

KATE: Yes, it was. I lied earlier. She wasn't even a very good cleaner.

HENRY: Do you miss him?

KATE: That reminds of the excellent country and western song: 'I still miss him, but my aim is getting better'.

HENRY: It must be by the same woman who wrote, 'I shaved my legs for this?'

KATE: Probably. I do miss him, but not as much as I thought I would. He needed someone to look up to him unquestioningly even when he wasn't in the pulpit. I think he might have been misled by seeing her doing the kitchen floor. I do worry that she'll be too clever for him as well.

HENRY: Where are they now?

KATE: Last I heard, running a b&b in Frinton on Sea.

HENRY: Frinton? I used to go there when I was a child.
KATE: I can see you as a little boy, Henry.
HENRY: I got lost there once, I remember. Frightening.

(Pause, more rattling train.)

MARTIN: *Clients may like to know that it's really pretty quiet in the buffet car, so, if you want to get your snacks and things, now would be a good time, as the lovely Kathleen here is very eager to serve you. Otherwise, Helga will be coming through with the trolley very shortly.*

(Sounds of people getting up and moving quickly towards the buffet car as the automatic door opens and closes very rapidly and repeatedly.)

HENRY: Now that's what I call a rush. I didn't expect the man in the blazer to be able to move like that, I must say. Didn't he have a pronounced limp earlier? No excuse for shoving that nun out of the way, though. I do hope we get to see Helga.
KATE: I'd like to see Martin. He's been strangely absent, except in a disembodied way. Is he hiding something? What do you think he looks like?
HENRY: I'm getting a combination of Huw Edwards, George Osborne and Barry Chuckle.
KATE: I'm thinking Wizard of Oz, when they find him behind the curtain. He'll be a very gnarled, small old man with a voice like Johnny Vegas.
MARTIN: *Hello, again, clients of mine, I shall be moving among you shortly to inspect your tickets, so prepare your best smiles and excuses. Just another little joke, as attempting to defraud the railway is an indictable*

offence punishable by several years imprisonment, and that's after Helga has had a word. That was a joke, Helga. Helga! Put him down! And no hiding in the lavs, either. That's not a joke. I have an axe. Pip-pip.

KATE: Is it me, or is this getting a bit weird?

HENRY: No, it's pretty normal for today. Depending on age and taste, people tend to blame it on Global warming, Mrs Simpson, Mrs Thatcher, Elvis, the end of National Service and the Grammar Schools, the 1960s, fluoridisation of the water, Princess Diana, the CIA, the rise of the ready meal, Tony Blair, the Treaty of Versailles or an international conspiracy involving crazed monks. It's actually about the democratisation of the celebrity culture, made inevitable by the demand for more television programmes and the lack of professional talent to meet it. Martin is clearly the star of his own reality programme and it no longer matters what the reality is. Hours of watching this sort of stuff have removed any power of independent action from us, so we just go along with it. I imagine Helga has a different perspective, but *you* can ask *her.*

KATE: So you're just going to go along with a crazed maniac with an axe running this train with his dangerous thug of a female accomplice? You're just going to sit there while we suffer a slow death between train-station-on-a-railway-line-momentary-stops-before-starting again? They may have started for all we know. Have you seen anyone come back yet?

HENRY: Now, I'm not going to say calm down, as I have learnt from experience that it can be a touch irritating, especially when followed by dear. But, come on, all we've got is a guard who fancies himself as a comedian, and a buffet attendant who seems to take a possibly excessive pride in her merchandise. Anyway, how do you know that chap didn't just have a nose bleed and was playing you along?

KATE: You didn't look into his eyes. The last time I saw somebody that frightened was when I told my ex-husband I had two tickets for the opera.

HENRY: I'll tell you what. I'll go and have a look and see if anything is going on as a gesture of our new friendship.

KATE: Thank you, Henry. I'd go myself, but I've got longer to live, and I'm terrified.

HENRY: Sometimes it's hard to be a woman. Sorry, sorry, there I am genuinely trying to sympathise and it comes out like one more feeble joke.

KATE: That's your defence against the world, Henry. Mine is appearing tougher than I am.

HENRY: All right, I'll go. But first I'm going to have my sandwich.

KATE: Oh, great. What's this, Sir Francis bloody Drake and his game of bowls? English sang-froid in the great tradition?

HENRY: Actually, I've often wondered why we don't have a word for sang-froid. Possibly because we know it's only a cover and that really we're just terrified of showing we're terrified. Which is why I want to eat my sandwich before Martin arrives, or, much more to the point, Helga.

(There is the sound of the automatic door opening and the clanking of a trolley. It is HELGA.)

KATE: Too late, mon brave!

HELGA: *(who is really quite a big woman with a heavy South African accent):* I'd put that sandwich down if I were you, sir.

HENRY: Don't be ridiculous! It's fish paste from a jar still in advance of its eat-before date opened earlier today and prepared by me after I'd washed my hands!

HELGA: We wouldn't want you to do anything silly, Sir, now would we? Just put the sandwich down. I've got a muffin.

HENRY: What nonsense! You'll be after my Dandelion & Burdock next!

HELGA: Dandelion & Burdock? Herbal stuff, is it, Sir? I think I'll have to take that too. European regulations.

HENRY: This is the last straw!

HELGA: Yes, I'll take that as well, please, Sir, filthy things.

MARTIN: *Hello, this is Martin again. Apologies for my no show re the tickets, but I've been been busy sorting out a misunderstanding between Kathleen and Sister Mary Magdalene involving the consumption of a Hot Bespoke British Bacon Baguette on a Friday. I promise you'll see me in the flesh – whoops, cheeky! – after our next train-station-momentary-stop, Churley, where we shall be arriving shortly.*

KATE: Excuse me, Churley is my stop. Would you mind moving your trolley?

HELGA: I'm not moving until I get those sandwiches and that suspicious-looking dark stuff. And the straw.

KATE: This is ridiculous. Do something, Henry.

HENRY: Oh, very well, here you are. Give me a muffin.

HELGA: I'm glad you've seen sense, Sir. We wouldn't have wanted any unfortunate little accidents, would we? Now, who's next? You, Sir, over there, was that a packet of caramel cremes you just put in your pocket?

(Sound of trolley moving on.)

MARTIN: *This is Churley, your railway line station momentary stop before starting again. This is Churley. Change here for Trumpton and Mornington Crescent but you must really want to change.*

KATE: Goodbye, Henry.

HENRY: Can I see you again?

KATE: No, Henry.

HENRY: Why not?

KATE: I think you know why not, Henry. When you bought that muffin something died.

HENRY: What do you mean? I thought you wanted me to buy the muffin!

KATE: The man I want wouldn't have bought the muffin. He would have found a way to eat his fish paste sandwich and vanquish that dreadful woman. He would have drunk his Dandelion & Burdock and made that noise when the straw hits the bottom and he would have made it triumphantly. I could see you again but we'd regret it. Maybe not today. Maybe not tomorrow, but soon and for the rest of our lives. Because there would be another muffin, there would be some other compromise, some other concession. You love the way the world was, Henry, but you're not prepared to fight for the good things that made it. Today a muffin, next month forget habeas corpus, detention without trial is absolutely fine, next month compulsory participation in Comic Relief. Goodbye, Henry.

(Sound of train doors slamming and the train starting again.)

HENRY: Damn, I've got something in my eye. Probably a bit of grit. *(Pause.)* I thought she didn't like fish paste sandwiches.

Scene Five...

MARTIN: *(who has a voice like Johnny Vegas)* Sir, Sir, wake up, please, Sir. Can I see your ticket, please, Sir?

HENRY: *(waking)* Yes, yes, sorry, here it is. Fell asleep. Had a very odd dream. Violence involving a blueberry muffin. A beautiful woman. A nun with a Hot Bespoke British Bacon Baguette. A driver with a pizza. I remember Adlestrop. Sorry, I'm babbling.

MARTIN: You've been a long way away.

HENRY: Yes.

MARTIN: Thank you for coming back to me. Here on the railways we are used to sleepers, if you follow my train of thought! *(Pause.)* Hmm. I'm afraid this ticket isn't valid for this service, though, sir.

HENRY: Not valid? What do you mean? It's a super super all day senior service summer season saver, isn't it?

MARTIN: Indeed it is, sir. But I think you'll find there isn't an R in the month. That'll be another, let me see, £4.99, sir, thank you.

HENRY: This is unbelievable!

MARTIN: Yes, it should be much more than £4.99. I don't how we do it, I really don't.

HENRY: Oh, all right, here you are!

MARTIN: I'm sorry, sir, we can't accept cards for sums less than £5.

HENRY: But I haven't got any cash! I spent the last of it one of your extortionately priced muffins! Here it is, take it back and give me a refund!

MARTIN: Extortion is an ugly word, sir. I'm afraid we cannot give a refund on food products once they have been handled by clients.

HENRY: But it's still inside its packet!

MARTIN: It's very crumbly, though, isn't it? You've obviously got a very strong grip. *(Pause)* That wrist watch looks like it's worth a bob or two.

HENRY: My watch?! This is outrageous!

MARTIN: All right, all right, sir, let's calm down, shall we? How about your mobile, then? Is it a smart phone? Have a think while I pop off to make an announcement.

HENRY: I don't believe this is happening!

ANOTHER PASSENGER: Shsssh! Quiet carriage!

HENRY: Oh, sorry. But, really!

MARTIN: *Hello, clients, this is Martin, your loveable etcetera, once again. We shall be be arriving at our final final full stop, Waterloo, in a little under, let me see, oh, I'd forgotten my watch has broken on me! Well, quite soon, anyway. Meanwhile this is a colleague announcement for Helga. Helga, would you like to join me in the Quiet Carriage to help resolve a small problem with a client who has become just a little over-excited during the exchange resolution cash shortfall procedure. Thank you.*

HENRY: My godfathers! Did you hear that, fellow travellers? Did you hear that shameless misrepresentation of the true position? That man is trying to diddle extra money out of me even though I have a perfectly valid ticket. And because I've spent all my spare cash on one of his wretched muffins, he's trying to get my watch off me. Well, there comes a moment when even the most civilised person cries hold and enough! When even the most reasonable of Englishmen realises that reasoning with the unreasonable is, well, unreasonable! Think of Alfred the Great, Hereward the Wake, and Robin Hood! Think of Cromwell and Churchill! They stood up to dictators! This bloody man and his crew can't even get the trains to run on time! I say we strike a blow today for the little man and woman, the lawn mowers, the cuttings takers, the door holders, the jam makers, the people of England who, in Chesterton's ringing words – that's G K Chesterton, 1874-1936 – have not spoken yet. What say you? Who's with me?

ENTIRE CARRIAGE: SSSHHHHH!

HENRY: No! For once I have raised my voice in the Quiet Carriage, and it will not be silenced! I will be heard, just as Paine and Wilkes and Wilberforce and Fry and Pankhurst were heard despite any amount of shushing. Think of Agincourt and Waterloo and Wembley, 1966! I say we seize this train and demand some proper service and respect, a maximum of three announcements a journey and a return to the British Rail standard pork pie!

(The sound of people getting up out of their seats, of bustle.)

HENRY: That's more like it! Follow me! Come on! Pause. Hey, where are you going?

ANOTHER PASSENGER: Waterloo. We're off.

(The sound of the train stopping and mass disembarkation. Then silence. Then the hiss of the carriage door and the clank of a trolley.)

Scene Six...

(The Quiet Carriage is now empty apart from Henry, Martin and Helga.)

HELGA: Ah, it's you again, is it, sir? I must say I didn't think much of the fish paste sandwiches. Less salt, if you know what's good for you.

MARTIN: This client, Helga, is refusing to acknowledge a debt he cannot settle by handing over an item of property as a certified guarantee, contrary to Section 219, Clause 112 of our terms and conditions.

HENRY: That's right. And if you are thinking of trying to take any such items by force I must warn you that I have dealt successfully in my time with both 3C on a Friday afternoon and a very large and angry man who was polishing the bonnet of his vintage Jaguar when Mr Arkinstall, one of my learners, was inadvertently in collision with it.

MARTIN: How on earth did he manage that?

HENRY: He mistook the man's drive for the B3016 to Finchampstead. Quite an easy thing to do, actually. Very narrow road, the B3016. I might not have been paying as much attention as I should, either. Can't say any more, ongoing and rather complex insurance claim.

HELGA: Well, we don't want any mistakes here, do we, sir? We wouldn't want the same thing to happen to you as happened to that chap who thought it would be so amusing to disrespect my muffins.

MARTIN: Your watch or your phone, please. Actually, both.

HENRY: You'll never get away with it!

MARTIN: That's what Sister Mary Magdalene said.

HENRY: What have you done with that old nun?

HELGA: She isn't a nun.

HENRY: Don't be ridiculous. I was educated by nuns when I was a nipper. I know what a nun looks like.

MARTIN: She has revealed in a frank discussion with Helga that she is in fact an undercover police officer specialising in food safety, illegal immigration and organised crime.

HENRY: That's a ridiculous combination. And she looks 80 if she's a day!

HELGA: That's how it is with undercover police officers today, Sir. Austerity has forced some elements of amalgamation and removed an upper age limit. Anyway, she's safe with Kathleen. There was more than bacon in that baguette.

HENRY: But Kathleen was refusing to give it to her!

MARTIN: Crafty, aren't we, sir? And ruthless.

HENRY: Well, fairly impressive, I suppose, if you're to be believed. How big is your organisation?

HELGA: Don't tell him, Martin!

MARTIN: What harm can it do? He's not going anywhere except the ultimate station stop, St Peter's Gate. We are an organisation dedicated to profit and disruption, masterminded by…*(Martin is interrupted by a dull thud)*…Aaagghh!

HELGA: I warned him!

HENRY: I've read about the Kosygin reverse pole axe but I never expected to see it!

HELGA: You're next, my friend!

MARTIN: *(Coming round)* What happened?

HENRY: Arrest this pair, officers!

HELGA: You don't expect me to fall for that old trick, do you?

MARTIN: What happened?

(The most tremendous kerfuffle, shouts of 'Got you, chummy!' and 'Don't try to escape, Miss!' and 'You'll never take me alive!', the sound of the trolley, winded grunts and crashing confectionery.)

Scene Seven…

HENRY: Where am I?

KATE: You're in hospital. You've had an exciting time.

HENRY: What happened?

KATE: Helga tried to barge her way out with the trolley. You flung yourself in the way and got knocked out.

HENRY: So that's why I've been dreaming I was run over by a giant muffin. I flung myself in front of the trolley? Did I?

KATE: Yes, rather heroic.

HENRY: Yes, it was, wasn't it?

KATE: Turns out Martin was another undercover policeman, wired for sound. We stumbled across the final act. Helga and her chums will be going down for a very long time. And Martin enjoyed it so much he's applied for a full-time position.

HENRY: Well, well, well. Guess we had old Martin figured wrong all along. But there's still one thing I don't understand.

KATE: What's that?

HENRY: What were you doing there?

KATE: Well, after I got off I started worrying about you.

HENRY: Worrying about me?

KATE: Yes. I knew really that under the wimpish exterior there beat the heart of a warrior. And I'd seen Helga. So I drove straight up here in time to scream as you went under the trolley. You ended up absolutely covered in muffin crumbs.

HENRY: Thank you, Kate. It's not quite James Bond, though, is it, being run over by a refreshment trolley?

KATE: A certain irony for a driving instructor, yes.

HENRY: By the way, you never answered. Before.

KATE: Never answered what?

HENRY: I asked you if you'd like to come up and see my trains.

KATE: So you did.

HENRY: Well?

KATE: I've been thinking. I don't really want to work for Russians. All those bodyguards, dark glasses, suits. But basically it's the decor. I'm

	not a bad driver, you know. You should have seen me on the way up to Waterloo. Perhaps I'll do some instructing as well.
HENRY:	What a team. I trust you indicated at roundabouts. *(Pause.)* There is something, though, that I ought to tell you first.
KATE:	What's that?
HENRY:	I do wear a driver's hat. With my trains.
KATE:	Toot! Toot!

With apologies and acknowledgements to Alfred Hitchcock, EH Thomas, Noel Coward, David Lean, Jimmy van Heusen, Johnny Mercer, Michael Flanders and Donald Swann.

WAY OUT SOUTH WEST +++

IT'S NOT BOLTON, thought Monthi Vaz, standing in the post office doorway and watching the village in its morning sunlight. Across from him stood the pub, which, after several name changes in pursuit of a more contemporary feel ('Rustico's', 'The Kick and Bucket', 'The Pub'), had now reverted to 'The Captain Pickering', after the local hero of a minor imperial skirmish with an excitable maharajah. The condition of the hanging baskets, always a reliable guide, suggested a waning enthusiasm.

An elderly woman appeared with a small dog that shared her passing resemblance to the late Margaret Rutherford. Both stopped to look at Monthi Vaz; one barked out a gruff greeting, the other just barked. 'Ow do', responded Monthi in friendly fashion, but dog and owner were already moving purposefully on, past the pub, the chemist, and what had once been the butcher's but was now a private house called, with typical rural middle-class jocularity, The Rotten Joint. Then they turned up through the lych gate into the graveyard of St Argha's and disappeared behind the church. Hallo, Combe Batzon, thought Monthi Vaz, turning the sign from closed to open: friendly bunch of buggers.

Still, early days. The first day, in fact; and not that long, really, since he had answered the advertisement. Monthi had been ready for a change even before his wife had run off with the confectionery and baked goods delivery driver. Bolton was all right, but it was his home town, and there was a limit to how often you could laugh at only moderately good Peter Kay impressions. Besides, he had just turned 30 and his mission to write the next great British Asian novel had run into the sands of disinspiration: it was partly his resulting distraction that had led his wife to seek hers amid the Battenbergs and the Garibaldis. Marta had told Monthi often enough that working in a corner shop wasn't exactly the height of her ambitions, but he hadn't taken enough notice, and certainly not of the confectionery and baked goods driver.

Still, there had been no children (possibly another sign of his lack of attention). And the change of scene, the quiet of the country and relaxed village hours would soon heal the hurt and lead to the triumphant completion of *The Brown Version,* a powerful tale of love and loss and family over several generations, islands and at least one sub-continent. Monthi had been interviewed for the job by Julia Pickering, daughter of Sir Frederick Pickering, descendant of the local hero, master of the Manor House (*'undistinguished', Pevsner*), owner of the post office, and widower. Julia, dark and lissom in that posh English way, ran a bijou catering company in London, and had been most taken with Monthi. 'God, you're just so right for this,' she said. 'High time Combe B really plunged into the multicultural swim. And you're from the North as well! So cool! Do say you'll come! Have you family?' Monthi, charmed but wary, said, 'No, not really. I'll be on my own.' Julia vaguely but swiftly wondered which Asian inter-sex tradition 'not really' might refer to, and decided against going there. 'Great, great! You'll be fine. Someone like you will make all the young marrieds from London feel quite at home. The locals will take a touch longer, but don't worry about their funny little ways, they're quite harmless, really. Pity Sebastian couldn't be here to show you the ropes. Poor Sebastian, it was very sudden. But Bess will be a great support, her family's been here for ever, she helps run the shop bit, so you'll need to get on the right side of her. And her cat, of course. Good old Hob. Slightly disconcerting stare, but you'll get used to that. The cat's got a bit of a look, too, but they'll be fine, don't worry. Now come and see the flat upstairs. You'll be used to being over the shop, won't you?'

'Oh, yes, it's in t'blood,' said Monthi, with a smile that transformed his usually serious face. 'First words I said were, "Owt else, luv?"'

Julia, recognising but not altogether following what she correctly took to be an example of the famous Northern sense of humour, laughed a little uncertainly but determinedly and led the way up to quarters which though compact had a fine view of The Captain Pickering and its sign, a side-whiskered soldier in a red coat which looked as if might be part of a not particularly distinguished job lot. 'That's my great-great-great-grandad,' said Julia. 'Pretty fierce by all accounts. He put down quite a few native rebellions with great gusto.' Then, remembering her audience, she added, 'Nothing personal, obviously. He killed quite a few round here as well.'

SO THAT HAD BEEN THAT, and here he was, Monthi Vaz, sub postmaster and village shop manager, Combe Batzon, Somerset, nestling in the Mendips, on his first morning and waiting for Bess, who was late. The door rattled open with a ping of its bell to reveal a youngish bald man whom Monthi recognised to be the vicar from his vicar's smile even before he noticed the dog collar inside the crumpled suit which had once had pretensions to imitate linen. 'Good morning, good morning,' beamed the Rev Gary Happie, vicar of St Aargha's, Combe Batzon and four others, including St Alric Agonistes, Deep Creech, and St Ubborn, Badley Chafing. 'I'm Gary,' he said, pointing brightly at the dog collar. 'God's Gift to Combe and surrounding parishes!'.

'Ow do, vicar,' said Monthi. 'Nice church'. 'Thank you. Pevsner wasn't too kind, I'm afraid. Clumsy buttresses, apparently.' The Rev Happie's voice trailed off as his face registered a thought. 'Sorry, when I say "God's Gift", I don't mean to be at all exclusive. My God is a God for all, not just an old fellow with a white beard for Anglicans on a Sunday, but one who looks upon and feels for all races, creeds and sexual preferences, no matter what the evangelicals might say. How are you settling in? I've not been here that long myself. Are you married? I think the nearest mosque must be in Trowbridge.'

Monthi Vaz smiled, not the open smile he had given Julia Pickering, but the polite, gently questioning smile he used for customers and anyone else under a misapprehension, whether about his religion or himself or the last second class post for Christmas. 'Bit early to say, vicar. First day today. But I'm not Muslim. I'm a Christian, of sorts: not your lot, Catholic, left-footer, non-practising.'

'Really,' said the vicar. 'Goa?'.

'Bolton,' said Monthi, who occasionally enjoyed employing the obtuseness which the natives seemed to expect from Asians. He knew that anyone of a liberal persuasion would be far too embarrassed by this response to inquire any further into his antecedents. But the vicar was right: his father's family was from Goa, the old Portuguese Indian colony which had somehow clung on until 1961. Zoze, Monthi's father, had arrived in Bolton, slightly mysteriously, to join the Gujaratis and Kashmiris working the dwindling night shifts in Lancashire's dying cotton mills because no one else would. 'There's safety in numbers, lad,' as he used to put it, before musing happily on various ironies, including Goa's consequent popularity as a cheap and cheerful retirement home for British pensioners. 'Round like a circle,' he would say, 'Like an ever whirring wheel'. For many years Monthi took this to be a piece of ancient eastern wisdom until Zoze revealed that it was in fact his approximation of some of the lyrics from the hit song, *Windmills of Your Mind*, by Noel Harrison, Rex's son. (Zoze only mentioned it so he could confide one of his prized collection of interesting local snippets, that sophisticated Rex had started out as a butcher's son from Huyton, near Liverpool. 'Yes,' Zoze said, happily, 'Old Rexy were a scouser!')

After the mills, Zoze had graduated to driving a taxi, then opened a corner shop before following his fathers to whatever paradise his hard labour and thick skin deserved. But not before insisting on his only son getting himself a good education. He had been less impressed by the anthropology degree from Manchester, confiding, whenever he could, that Monthi should 'stand behind this counter and you'll get all bloody anthropology you need'. Which is what happened, temporarily at first, when Monthi discovered how little call there was for anthropologists who had ambitions beyond soliciting with clipboards in unfriendly shopping centres or telephoning unannounced to inquire about attitudes to spin driers. Monthi's mother was unrecalled by him except in the most shadowy way. 'She were a Parsee,' was all his father would say, 'And she passed'. So, nominally a Catholic, with a fire-worshipper for a mother, if Zoze was to be believed, which he wasn't, always. Quite a lot to communicate, even if he had wanted to; and the vicar was now proffering a copy of The Guardian. ('Only one copy of the Guardian, my lover. Always a bit of a race between the vicar and Sir Frederick,' the man who delivered the newspapers had said earlier, employing the local term of endearment in the slow Somerset burr that took some getting used to even if you weren't from Bolton. Monthi had wondered why they couldn't have two, even three, copies. The man had looked at him oddly: 'Where would the fun be in that?').

The vicar departed, mentioning over his shoulder something about 'outreach' and 'a journey' which was lost in the door-opening and bell-ringing. Some time passed before the arrival of what could only be Bess, as she was glowering and accompanied by a very large, irritable-looking cat.

'You must be Bess,' said Monthi.

'Must I?', said Bess. 'You the new post man, then?'

'Postmaster,' Monthi corrected, politely. 'And I don't think we can have that cat in here. Foodstuffs, you know.'

'Sebastian used to let me have Hob in here,' said Bess, pausing before adding, 'Fat lot of good it did him'.

She took off her heavy coat, hung it up in the store room that led off from the counter area, and shooed Hob out with affront. Hob jumped up on the outside window sill and stared in unwaveringly at Monthi, who had retreated into his glass post office booth, and was pretending to be busy loading his stamp machine. Bess stared at him from behind the counter. She was vigorously rubbing her thumb and middle finger together. Monthi was intrigued by this, as he recognised it to be a gesture employed in parts of Turkestan against the Evil Eye.

The silence was broken, eventually, by a disturbingly loud squeal from Hob, followed immediately by the door and the bell combination. A large man entered, walked to the newspaper stand and complained loudly, 'Bloody vicar's got it! How am I going to read Polly's piffle now? Hello, Bess. That cat's slowing down a bit, isn't he?' Sir Frederick looked nothing like his ancestor outside the pub, favouring instead a striking resemblance to an angry Bill Clinton in tweed. He noticed Monthi Vaz behind the glass, frowned then smiled, which, owing to the size of his teeth, wasn't reassuring. 'You must be the new chap! Settling in all right?' He gestured towards Bess, who had remained impassive: 'Keep an eye on this old witch. Terrible woman, aren't you, Bess?'

'Very good, Sir Frederick,' said Bess, without enthusiasm.

'The nearest mosque's in Trowbridge,' continued Sir Frederick. 'Any chance of fifty quid?'

Monthi, wearing the polite smile, said, 'Bit early to tell, but thanks.' He decided against entering into another theological discussion and moved swiftly on to the transaction, 'Can I have your card?'.

'Card?', said Sir Frederick. 'I haven't got one. Everyone knows who I am. I'm Frederick Pickering. Don't need a card, for heaven's sake. Next thing you'll be asking for my phone number'.

'No, sorry, I mean your bank card. For the £50,' said Monthi, still calm and trained by any number of encounters with Bolton pensioners.

'Ah,' said Sir Frederick. 'Misunderstood you there. I own the post office, you see. Just a matter of handing over the cash in tenners.'

Monthi, less calm, said, 'No, I can't do that. It doesn't work like that. It's the Royal Mail's money.'

'Ah,' said Sir Frederick. 'Worth a try. Well done. On the ball. What's your name again?'

'Monthi. Monthi Vaz,' said Monthi.

'Excellent. We'll call you Mike. Must dash, got to see a tenant about an eviction. *Hasta la vista*, Bess, keep your bowels open'.

Monthi was now beginning to entertain serious doubts about the creative tranquility required to complete *The Brown Version*. Still, the rest of his first day went more smoothly. Some customers would be too studiously normal; others, women with loud voices and glasses worn as Alice bands, men with loud voices and trousers, both often with irritating children, would be over-hearty; and others, whom Monthi took to be the indigenous population, stared at him, and then stared at Bess, who stared back. His cheerful greeting of ''Ow do, luv,' seemed to endear him to none of these groups, so Monty decided to turn down the Lancashire charm, recognising a structural resistance that would have to be overcome gradually.

He was also wryly aware that anthropology in Britain had begun in Bolton before the Second World War with the work of the Mass Observation group, outsiders who had arrived to study the habits of Boltonians as if they were a foreign tribe. The detail he had always liked best was that these Southerners (toffs!) used to play George Formby records in their rented house to get into the swing of things. They had conducted their research by eavesdropping, never directly questioning, so as to keep the research unmediated by their interjection. Monthi was reminded of the force of the method in the post office: the indigenes were talking to him slowly, solemnly and loudly, but cackling and joshing with Bess, who seemed to entertain them hugely without changing expression. Sadly, his research was hampered by Bess's low murmur and the glass of his booth, although he was pretty sure he heard 'Mecca', 'how many virgins?', 'That Solomon Rushdie' and 'I couldn't live without a bacon sandwich, no way'. Monthi closed his booth for lunch, went over to the chilled counter and selected one of the snacks. He took it to Bess and carefully paid out the correct money. 'I don't know about you,' he announced loudly, 'but I do like a pork pie.'

He ate the pie, of best filling-station quality, on a seat under the big oak tree at one side of the lazy oblong that passed as Combe's village square. There was an inscription on the bench that read, 'In Memory of Gordon Demdike. He loved this spot as much as anywhere.'

Sir Frederick emerged from The Captain Pickering, spotted Monthi, and came over. 'Mike, hello. How's it hanging? Just been in the Pick for a heart-starter. Don't suppose you drink, though, do you?' 'Not at lunchtime, no,' said Monthi. 'Thought not,' said Sir Frederick. He pointed at the inscription on the bench. 'Bess's husband,' he said. 'Morose chap, unsurprisingly. Don't think I ever heard him speak. Bad squint. Went very suddenly. Must dash, arrears to extract.'

MONTHI FOUND HE HAD developed a slight headache. He went back into the post office and asked Bess for some painkillers. 'Don't sell them,' said Bess. 'Just boil up some Monkshood, that'll sort you out'.

'Monkshood?'

'Yes, it's growing for free all round. Lilac coloured flowers. Very good for headaches, but be a bit careful with the dose, as it can kill you.'

'Hmmm,' said Monthi. 'Wouldn't it be a good idea if we did stock some analgesics or whatever?'

'Sebastian came to an understanding with the chemist,' said Bess. 'We wouldn't sell them if he didn't sell milk.'

'Milk?' said Monthi, 'At a chemist? Not a bad deal for him, then.'

'Ah, well, see, Sebastian liked him. Milk does seem to curdle very quickly in here, though.'

Bess had become almost voluble; Monthi, encouraged, mentioned the seat, said it was a fine tribute and told her he was sorry for her loss. 'I didn't pay for it,' said Bess. 'Sir Frederick did. I wasn't fussed myself. But he said it would be a fitting tribute and he needed somewhere to put the bench because Julia was installing "some bloody Nip tranquility garden," up at the Manor, if I remember him right. Proper job, though, big concrete plinth, him'll never shift. Bit like Gordon, idle old sod.' Bess went into the store room and emerged in her coat. 'I'll be off now,' she said. '

'Old up,' said Monthi. 'Who's going to serve while I'm behind here?'

Don't you worry about that,' said Bess. 'Felt making workshop in the village hall and *Murder She Wrote* at three. There'll be no-one in.' She left with Hob, who had materialised from somewhere, slouching along behind. Bess was right. Monthi spent most of the rest of the afternoon studying the eccentric stock list – rubber bands, cocktail sausage sticks, pink polkadot fairy-cake cases – and familiarising himself with the latest fiendish device the Royal Mail had come up with to complicate the posting process, an inflatable categorisation carton which deployed a range of flashing lights and piercing beeps to advise if a parcel was too big or heavy for the more economically advantageous dispatch option. None of this, particularly the inflation of the categorisation carton, helped Monthi's headache. After the day's mail had been collected by a taciturn Royal Mail person – 'You're Sebastian's successor, are you? Good luck' – he closed up and hurried over to the chemist.

A small, very neat man with very neat grey hair in a very white coat was standing behind the counter in the otherwise empty chemist's. Monthi, forewarned by previous experience, decided to substitute ' 'Allo there,' for 'Ow do'. 'I'm the new postmaster and I need something for a headache'.

'I'm not surprised,' said the chemist in an unexpected accent.

'Polish, eh?' said Monty. 'Been here long?'

The chemist sighed. 'Long enough. And I am not Polish,' he said.'Nor would I assume where you were from, although Bolton would be my choice if you insisted. What kind of analgesic do you require?'

'Sorry,' said Monthi. 'It's my first day and I don't seem to be doing very well. And I've got this throbbing pain in the back of my head. What do you recommend?'

'I would recommend in the immediate instance, paracetamol, as it has the fewest side effects. In the longer term, I would not be the postmaster in Combe Batzon.'

'Well, that's clear, anyway. What's it like being a chemist in Combe Batzon?'

'Not especially rewarding in either financial, pastoral or professional terms. But beggars, or rather Eastern Europeans with pre-1990 medical qualifications, cannot be choosers. Here you are. That will be £1. Would you like a glass of water?'

Monthi paid and took a glass of water, gratefully, and downed two pills. 'Thanks. I'm Monthi Vaz. You?'

'My name is Stanislav Novak, though of course everyone round here calls me Steve. And now if you will excuse me, I'm closing.'

'Of course. Don't suppose you fancy a swift stress-buster next door? Unless you wouldn't advise alcohol with paracetemol.'

'There are no known interactions between alcohol and paracetamol. I shall join you for a drink. I should like a dry sherry.'

'I'd have thought you'd be on Slivovitz.'

'There you go again. Slivovitz is too sweet for me, and something of a cliché. I prefer Pelinkovec, which has a bracingly bitter edge to it, and being based on wormwood, also affords excellent protection against malaria.'

'Surely there's no malaria round here?'

'That's why I'm having a dry sherry'.

Stanislav had now locked up his shop. They made their way to The Captain Pickering. The pub's interior was dark and empty except for a man who was resting his head on his crossed arms, asleep, on a table near the bar. 'Good evening, Sidney,' said Stanislav. The man stirred, rubbed his face and said, in a tone of voice familiar to all who have encountered the traditional English landlord, 'What's good about it?'. He got up and went behind the bar, from where he stared at them, balefully.

'Ay up,' said Monthi, re-introducing and accentuating the northernness, as he tended to do in challenging masculine circumstances. 'Two pints of best bitter, please.' 'We've only got one bitter,' said Sidney, jabbing his finger at the pump, which had a roughly handwritten sign on it reading 'Bitter'. 'Reet, reet, two pints of that, then, please,' said Monthi. 'Have you got any peanuts?' Sidney jabbed at another handwritten sign, which looked as if it had been on the wall for some time. 'Kitchen closed owing to staff shortage'. 'Reet, thanks,' said Monthi, retreating towards the far corner where Stanislav was sitting.

'Friendly sort of fellow,' said Monthi, taking a sip. 'Mmm. Not bad, actually.' 'You're supposed to say something disobliging,' said Stanislav. 'Your being a Northerner and it being Southern beer'.

'Listen, I were brought up on Greenall Whitley, lad. And most people don't think any Asian should be drinking, let alone know anything about it. I'm a Christian by birth, as it happens, but the natives never seem able to get their heads round that, they think it isn't allowed for a brown person.'

'You think you've got it bad? I'm a Bosnian Muslim.'

'Seriously? You're not!'

'No, I'm a Slovenian, but occasionally I attempt an English joke.'

'Slovenia. Some very interesting spring rites, burning corn dollies and St George as the Green Man. I studied anthropology at university. I've also read that it's unlucky to see an elephant in Slovenia, but I'm not sure about that.'

'I'm a man of science, so forgive me if I'm not quite so well acquainted with our national superstitions as you. I should have thought you'd have to be quite lucky to see an elephant in Slovenia, but I left a few years ago. I like the idea of an anthropologist as the post master in an English village, though. Will you be publishing a study?'

'I suppose it depends if I need to keep the job. I'm writing a novel.'

'Neither am I. That's another English joke, laden with English nervousness in the face of anything remotely intellectual. But with me, it's true: I'm not writing a book. But I do watch the natives. Sidney here, for example, has been even more misanthropic since his wife left a couple of months ago.'

'Ran off with the pot man, did she?' said Monthi, for whom such things still rankled. 'No,' said Stanislav, 'She just disappeared'.

'Perhaps she went off with Sebastian. Who is Sebastian? Or who was Sebastian?'

'Sebastian Pickering, Sir Frederick's son and heir, late part-time postmaster, full-time drinker and disaster, and recent escapee. But he's unlikely to have run off with Mrs Sidney, as he's gay.'

'Oh, I see. The only gay in the village?'

'No. There's also me.'

'Oh, sorry, I didn't realise.'

'Don't apologise. I didn't realise myself until I met Nigel on my UK pharmacy qualification course. There was, if you'll forgive the pun, chemistry between us. But let me get you another one.'

Stanislav approached the bar. 'Same again, I suppose, Steve?' said Sidney, with a sigh. The pub door opened; it was the woman resembling Margaret Rutherford whom Monthi had half-met first thing in the morning. 'Stay, Putin, stay!' she called over her shoulder. She nodded to Stanislav, 'Steve,' she said, with a deliberate emphasis on the incongruity of name and subject. 'Usual when you're ready, Sidney.' she said. Stanislav brought the drinks over. The woman picked up the glass of *creme-de-menthe* Sidney had grudgingly poured for her, swallowed it in one gulp, paid out some coins on to the bar, turned on her sensible heel and walked out again, nodding to Monthi as she left.

'She keeps on the move, doesn't she?' said Monthi. 'I sort of met her this morning, but she didn't really stop then, either.'

'Tradecraft, probably,' said Stanislav. 'The local intelligence is that she's a retired MI6 officer, Dorothy-Anne Marjoribanks. Still convinced I'm an agent, hence her way with my name.'

'Bloody 'ell,' said Monthi. 'I should have done a bit more research on this place before taking the job. There's some odd sods round here, aren't there? We seem about the most normal.'

'Comparisons are rarely instructive. Some might say that was the essential mistake of Communism. In any event, wherever Nigel and I chose to set up shop was almost certain to regard us as abnormal. Gay immigrant. Right up there on the UKIP hit list, along with aid workers and straight bananas.'

'Nigel says a lot, too. Do you know the Welsh used to refer to the England rugby team as the Nigels? But it could have been worse. You could have been brown'.

'You could have been a Muslim.'

'Everyone thinks I am, anyway. And it can be handy. I quite often get a seat on public transport, for example.'

'So why didn't you do any research before coming here? At least Nigel knew Sebastian, who marked our card. West country, broadly tolerant, unless you're a gypsy.'

'Ah, yes, the age-old tension between settler and traveller, ant and grasshopper. The farmer and the cowboy should be friends, that sort of thing. Well, like I said, I've got this novel to finish, and I'm in a hurry. Oh, and there I go forgetting, my wife ran off with the confectionery and baked goods delivery driver.'

'Well, she showed more taste than Nigel, who ran off with the condom salesman.'

'Another English joke?'

'Sadly not. Yours?'

'Sadly not, although it sounds like one. Marta is from Cartagena and Frank Mather, the bastard, is from Wigan, so at least I'm doing my bit for integration.'

'Interestingly, the condom salesman is a prick from Barnsley.'

There was, as you might expect, a period of silence after this exchange, broken by Monthi saying, 'Interesting decor in here.'

'The key point, I have found,' said Stanislav. 'Is whether the ornamentation is knowing. In this case, it's not.' Some other drinkers were now arriving, mostly distinguished by the length of the stare they devoted to Monthi before settling on the more familiar middle distance.

'Why did you say being postmaster here would be bad for my health?'

'It got Sebastian down, that's why he suddenly disappeared, if you ask me, and as long as you are fully aware it is only a conjecture. His father is completely impossible. Has he tried to get any money out of you yet? He's like a small boy in a sweet shop, made worse by his invincible conviction that he has invincible charm. And then there's Bess.'

'Ah, yes, Bess. I'm going to have to study her a bit further, but I'm pretty sure she's a witch.'

'She's certainly bewitched Sir Frederick. They've been lovers for years.'

'Bloody 'ell,' said Monthi. 'Bloody 'ell. I didn't see that one coming. She's not exactly what you'd call conventionally attractive, is she?'

'Who knows with the English. Sex for them seems rather more complicated than for the rest of us. What's the anthropological view?'

'It's complicated, but basically it's down to the successive invasions of the island: the differing approaches to sex of the Italians, Germans, and Vikings caused enough confusion without the arrival of French Vikings, which is essentially what the Normans were. This lack of consensus, particularly in matters of technique and courting ritual, led to a lack of confidence which in turn led to the Empire and all this sport as distractions to avoid embarrassment.'

'So that's why they find modern immigration so threatening?'

'Yes. They rightly suspect that we are all superior lovers.'

'How does that tie in with your Frank and my Nigel?'

'I'm still working on that,' said Monthi Vaz.

THE NEXT FEW weeks fell into a pattern. The post office had its busy times, but at others, particularly in the afternoons, there was little business for the Royal Mail or the rude greetings cards, tins of soup, novelty pens, pies, moth balls, combs, sweets with unfamiliar labels and books of varied and varying local interest that formed the remainder of the shop's stock along with the rubber bands and the rest. At these times, always predicted with complete accuracy by Bess, Monthi began looking at *The Brown Version* again, finding some of it not half bad, some of it all bad. The love interest for the hero of the contemporary section seemed especially uninspired. When he mentioned this to Stanislav at one of their now regular early evening drinks in The Captain Pickering, his new friend said, 'I fear your unpleasant experience in the confectionery area is still too fresh. I myself have never liked the Battenberg cake. Smacks too much of central European hegemonies. You should try *Prekmurska gibanica*, Slovenian layer cake. The dough is sprinkled with cabbage or turnip. Delicious, but far too sophisticated for English tastes. They can't see beyond the carrot.'

The love life of Sir Frederick and Bess, in contrast, was fascinating. Sir Frederick continued his daily visits, but Monthi could discern nothing between them beyond what passed as a pleasantry for Sir Frederick – 'Having your broomstick serviced today, my dear?' – and the tersest of barely polite acknowledgements from Bess. Monthi, too, was still having difficulty working out the mutual attraction. 'They used to say much the same about Edward VIII and Mrs Simpson,' said Stanislav. 'H G Wells, although no beauty, was supposed to possess a body odour that made him irresistible to women. The H G Wells cocktail is anise based. Does Bess eat fennel?'

'Interesting,' said Monthi. 'The Benandanti, a 16th Century Italian sect who believed they could travel out of their bodies, were very keen on fennel. Some cultures believe it protects against meddlers.'

'Hmm,' said Stanislav. 'There are some herbal treatments that use it as a cure for flatulence. It does have quite a strong smell. You could always sniff her.'

Sidney took their empty glasses without comment. There was still no sign of Mrs Sidney, and the hanging baskets were now in some distress. 'Can't think what's happened to the cow,' confided Sidney at regular intervals. 'You'd think she'd be grateful, but no, upped and gone. Gone from me, after all I'd done for her.' Sidney hitched his trousers and idly scratched under his arm. Monthi thought of suggesting fennel, but didn't. 'She couldn't have had any complaints in the bedroom department,' continued Sidney, with a belch that also invited thoughts of the helpful green herb. 'A complete mystery,' he said.

'Grateful?' said Monthi to Stanislav outside the pub. 'Grateful to Sidney?'

'Ah,' said Stanislav. 'I might have omitted to mention that Mrs Sidney was a Thai bride, and so in Sidney's eyes bound tighter to him than his shirt around his midriff, it being a transaction involving things more important than love.'

'Bloody 'ell,' said Monthi. 'And Julia said I would be introducing multi-culturalism to Combe Batzon.'

'Well, to be fair, I'm white and we didn't see much of Mrs Sidney. He didn't let her out very often.'

'He's a hard man to like, Sidney, isn't he?' said Monthi.

'I don't try,' said Stanislav Novak. In Slovenia, we have a saying, "Vsak je svoje sreče kovač." It translates approximately as "Each man is the smith of his own fortune."

"Excellent," said Monthi. "I'm very keen on proverbs. There's a Goan one I've always liked, "Fry the chapati when the pan is hot". It applies to most situations, I find.'

'Yes, that is good,' said Stanislav. 'Slovenian sayings can be more direct. For example, in regard to getting other people to do things you don't want to do yourself, we say, "It's always easier to beat the poison ivy with someone else's dick."'

They were now walking away from the pub. As Stanislav confided his second piece of Slovenian wisdom, Miss Marjoribanks came round the corner with Putin, who was panting, unattractively. 'Very good, Mr Novak,' she said. 'That reminds me of a saying we used to have in my line of work – "Stand close to the tree if you want to squeeze the plums". Miss Marjoribanks moved briskly on, Putin wheezing behind.

'That sounded a bit painful,' said Monthi. 'She looks like she might enjoy squeezing plums. Or was it an oblique reference to Slivovitz?'

'Slovenians also say that no one is obtuse without a reason. And now I am going home to read our most famous philosopher, Slavoj Zizek, who can also seem remarkably obtuse but is in fact quite clear, as in his oft-quoted contention that, "Ultimately, we hear things because we cannot see everything". Goodnight, Monthi.'

Monthi, still smiling at having found such a friend, walked over to the post office. As he was putting his key into the flat's front door, round the side, he looked back and saw Miss Marjoribanks had stopped and was writing in a small notebook while Putin squatted next to her, his face grimacing in concentration, taking the same approach to the pavement that his namesake tended to adopt towards his neighbours.

HOB SCREAMED, the door opened and the bell rang. It was, force of naturally, Sir Frederick. He addressed Monthi and Bess over his shoulder as he strode to the newspaper rack. 'Morning, Mike,' he said, 'Morning, your ladyship. Gotcha!'. The latter accompanied his seizure of The Guardian. 'Can't have the vicar corrupted any further. Besides, my life is otherwise lacking in strong women of earnest views who are not afraid to share them, eh, Bess?' Bess, as impassive as ever, said, 'Very good, Sir

Frederick,' while making a gesture which looked remarkably to Monthi like the sign of the cross in reverse. 'Oh, Mike, Julia's up at the Manor. She said you might pop in for lunch if you're not otherwise engaged.' Monthi thought this a very good idea, and said so. 'Good, good,' said Sir Frederick. 'Any change in your monetary policy?'

'If you mean giving you money, Sir Frederick, I'm afraid not,' said Monthi. 'But we've got a very keen exchange price on Bulgarian Lev.'

'Never heard of the fellow,' said Sir Frederick.

'Very good, Sir Frederick,' said Monthi.

A few hours later Monthi, rather more excited than he cared to concede, was up at the Manor House. He could see why Pevsner had been sniffy, but it did have that English solidity which he admired, even though he was often exasperated by the accompanying lack of spark, the complacency that the kind would call smug and the unkind stupidity. The heavens, Monthi and Pevsner knew that Bolton and Lancashire lacked some of the obvious attraction of the Mendips, but there was more life there, fizzed by the waves of immigrants which had begun during the Industrial Revolution and continued ever since, right up to and beyond the House of Vaz. As his father had been fond of saying, 'You tell me anywhere else that has played host to Sigmund Freud, the Mahatma Gandhi, Adolf Hitler and Zoze Vaz' (even though Hitler, in Liverpool, in 1912, staying with his half-brother, was, Zoze would concede, when pressed, only circumstantial). Mind you, thought Monthi, as he contemplated the scrawled message on the front door of the Manor House advising anyone other than the Pope to go round to the back, Combe Batzon was not entirely unstimulating.

Julia answered the back door, as elegant and unstudied as he remembered. 'Monthi! Come in!' They made their way through a number of large, frayed but surprisingly tidy rooms to the kitchen. 'Tomato soup ok for you?' asked Julia.

'Aye, if you're opening a tin,' said Monthi, as a joke, before Julia started to do just that.

'Cook's day off,' said Julia.

'I didn't know you had a cook,' said Monthi.

'Well, actually, it's been cook's day off for about five years now, when Bess left. To be honest, we've all felt a lot better ever since'.

Monthi paused to assimilate this startling piece of information. 'I thought you ran a catering company,' he said.

'Oh, I don't cook as such,' said Julia. 'I have a number of very talented people who do that for me. Which leads me to the specific reason I wanted to see you, besides finding out how you're getting on, of course.'

'Well, I'm afraid I have a pretty limited repertoire,' said Monthi. 'Hotpot or Sorpotel, mainly.'

'Sorpotel?'

'Pork liver, tongue and blood curry, excellent.'

'Pork? I thought, you know,' said Julia, tailing off and vaguely wafting the arm that wasn't stirring the soup.

'No, my family's from Goa, said Monthi, getting more Lancastrian. 'Born a Catholic, me. I were impressed by the welcome for the Pope on the front door.'

'You're Catholic!? How marvellous! We were Catholics, but my great grandfather gave it up when Evelyn Waugh came over. Lowered the tone rather, like that gloomy Graham Greene. Daddy wrote that note. You've probably experienced his sense of humour by now. But it wasn't cooking I wanted to talk about, although I suppose it is in a roundabout way.' Julia served up the soup without adornment and gave up the hunt for some bread. 'Sorry, not wonderful, is it?' she said, pushing her dark hair up off her forehead and giving Monthi a smile that set off a curious tingling in all parts Vaz, north, east, west and particularly south. 'Actually, I was after a bit of a favour, well a large one, really. Don't let your soup go cold.'

Monthi blinked, smiled and took a spoonful. 'What is it, then, this favour?' he asked. Julia opened her eyes wider. Monthi wondered how he hadn't noticed their stunningly fine flecked amber before.

'You know The Captain Pickering, don't you? Daddy says you're in there quite regularly with the Polish Chemist. But I can tell him to stop muttering now we know you're a Catholic. Anyway, you must know Sidney. Dear Sidney. Have you met Mrs Sidney?'

'No, she seems to have disappeared before I arrived. I understand she's a Thai lady. And Stanislav is a Slovene.'

'Slow Bean? Is it a local dish?'

'No, sorry, that's my accent. Stanislav is from Slovenia, not Poland.'

'Sorry, sorry, silly me. Daddy again, I'm afraid.' Julia's embarrassed laugh, followed by another appealing look, would have disarmed Monthi if he hadn't been disarmed already. 'The thing is, Monthi, that Pakpao, or Pat, as everybody calls her, is a fantastic cook. The food at the Pick was exceptional while she was there. But Sidney was more than a mite possessive, as you've probably heard, and not the most gracious of men, as you've probably seen, and she wanted – needed – to get away. So that's why she's working for me now in London.'

'Well, I'll go to the foot of our stairs,' said Monthi. 'Nobody else seems to know that.'

'No, they wouldn't. It was a discreet girls' thing.'

'Excuse my curiosity, but while we're on missing persons, what about Sebastian?'

'I'm not sure about Sebastian, to be honest. Daddy knows more than he's letting on, certainly to me.' Julia gave Monthi a glance that managed to combine hurt, vulnerability, pluckiness and a deep need to be comforted. Julia, he felt, at this moment, tomato soup growing cold and congealing slightly, could ask him to do anything, anything at all.

'So I was wondering,' she said, 'If you could break into the Pick for me.'

'SORRY?' SAID MONTHI. 'Do you know, for a moment there, I thought you were asking me to break into the Pick'.

'I am. Pat left her suitcase there so as not to make Sidney suspicious. It's got some of her most precious clothes and possessions in it and she's beginning to pine for them. Frankly, it's having an effect on her cooking. All you'd have to do is to get in the back while Sidney's serving and grab the suitcase, which is on top of the wardrobe in their bedroom. It wouldn't take a minute.'

Julia was giving him that look again; and there was no finer tribute to it than that Monthi Vaz, sensible sub-postmaster, sensibly detached anthropologist, a man whose previous record in shadiness extended no further than not paying his fare that time on the 22 to Ince aged 11, was seriously considering breaking and entering. 'Why me?' he asked, trying to sound relaxed, a man of the world.

'You're from the North,' said Julia. 'And I was trying to think of someone I could trust round here, someone I could rely on to be efficient yet discreet, sensitive yet ruthless, and my search soon stopped at you, Monthi.'

The way Julia lingered over 'efficient', 'discreet', 'sensitive', and, especially, 'ruthless', left Monthi with no choice. 'Ok. Leave it with me,' he said, instantly wishing he could have come up with something a little less middle- managerial, more no-nonsense man of Bolton and action.

Julia seemed pleased, though. 'I knew you wouldn't let me down!' she cried. 'More soup?'

'I DON'T SEE WHY it shouldn't work,' said Stanislav. 'He's hardly the most alert of men, is he? If necessary, I could keep him occupied with what the English call banter, which, as I understand it, seems mostly to consist of prejudiced remarks delivered with a knowing smile inviting complicity. It might be diverting, but I'm still unsure why you want to do it, unless it's the attractions of the beautiful Julia.'

'Got it in one, Stanislav. She has a wonderfully strange effect on me. I was very fond of Marta, at least until Frank bloody Mather arrived with his cakes and smarm, but this is different. Julia makes me feel 16 again. You've no idea how much it's perked up my novel.'

Stanislav took a sip of sherry, and began to whistle a tune, slightly tunelessly, it must be said. "What is that?" said Monthi. "I know I know it. It's Sinatra, isn't it? Go on, tell me."

'*Witchcraft, Wicked Witchcraft*,' said Stanislav.

Dusk the next evening found Stanislav Novak at the bar of The Captain Pickering and Monthi Vaz entering by the back door and through another marked private which he assumed would lead, eventually, to Sidney's master bedroom. In this he was correct, particularly about eventually. He had no idea that one pub could have so many upstairs rooms in such a state of disarray with such creaky floors. Downstairs, even Sidney seemed to be noticing the odd sound, despite being in the middle of explaining to Stanislav exactly what was wrong with most things. The pub being empty thanks to the cumulative effect of the deserted Sidney didn't help, either. When he broke off after another bump just above them, Stanislav was forced to play his trump and wonder aloud why there were so many Thai restaurants in Britain.

Monthi had now gained the bedroom, and could indeed see the suitcase on top of the wardrobe. What complicated things was that it was one of two, one on top of the other. Monthi, on the tippiest of tip toes, slid the top one off into his hands, juggling frenziedly as the lid flew open, neatly depositing a black hat on to his head before he got the case under control and put it on the bed. The remainder of the contents included a black mask, black shirt, a black plastic rapier and a pair of black trousers with, he couldn't help noticing even in his travails, an interesting crotch arrangement. 'Well, well,' thought Monthi, giggling despite himself, 'Zorro! Good old Sidney! No wonder Pat buggered off.' He went back for the next suitcase, and was just sliding it off when he noticed himself in the wardrobe mirror still wearing the hat. He started back and the wardrobe door swung open, knocking him off balance and back onto the bed.

Sidney broke off from explaining that a lot of these Thais were actually Chinese masquerading as Thais, just like a lot of apparently Italian waiters were actually Hungarian, you just couldn't trust anybody, especially Thais, look at Pat, he'd given her everything. 'What was that?!' he shouted. 'Someone's upstairs!'. With an agility that did very little to suggest the legendary Latin American superhero, Sidney set off at an agitated waddle to investigate. Monthi, meanwhile, realising from the agitation below that his means of entry was now blocked, made for the window with Pat's suitcase, pausing only, with a presence of mind that came as a surprise, to put on the Zorro mask. Luckily, the bedroom was above The Captain Pickering's single-storey toilet block, and Monthi was able to lower himself down on to it. He was just about to get down to the ground when he heard a noise that gave him fresh insight into a word rather over-used in certain types of fiction: bloodcurdling.

Peering down, he saw Putin, who was looking up at him, growling ominously, and, almost certainly, although it was now too dark to make it out properly, slavering. The light in the bedroom had gone on: Monthi had no choice but to pray that jumping down would frighten off Putin. He jumped.

Unfortunately, Putin chose that moment to move towards where Monthi was landing, and the postmaster caught the dog a glancing blow with Pat's suitcase as he hit the grass and staggered to keep his balance. At this point, Stanislav arrived. Monthi had never heard Stanislav giggle before. 'It's not funny,' he hissed. 'It is,' said Stanislav. Above them, they could hear Sidney shouting out of the window, 'Is that you, Pat? What have you done with my outfit?' Up on the square, they could also now hear an approaching Miss Marjoribanks: 'Putin! Putin! Where are you?'

Stanislav gingerly prodded Putin, who was lying still on the grass, with his foot. 'Good boy, Putin,' he whispered, 'Go to your mistress.' Putin didn't move.

'Trapped!' said Monthi.

'My God! It's Antonio bloody Banderas!' said Sir Frederick, who had come out of the Pick by the back way, and fainted.

'Freddie!' cried Bess, who had appeared from nowhere. Hob approached the prone Putin, who promptly got to his paws and fled towards Miss Marjoribanks.

'I would advise against any sudden movements,' said the vicar, who was standing behind Sir Frederick and Bess holding a Walther P99 automatic pistol.

'Well, I wasn't expecting that,' said Miss Marjoribanks.

'I DON'T KNOW about anybody else,' said Stanislav. 'But I could do with a drink. Why don't we all go inside and discuss whatever's going on calmly and sensibly?'

'I've no objection to that,' said the vicar, in even tones. 'Providing everyone – and that includes you up there, Sidney – understands that that my first shot will be fatal rather than a warning.'

'Bloody Guardian reader,' said Sir Frederick, who had now been helped by Bess to his feet. They moved inside as a group and sat round a table, guarded by the vicar.

'Give everyone a drink, please, Sidney,' said Stanislav. Sidney looked at the vicar, who nodded.

'On the house, I would suggest, Sidney,' said Monthi.

Reluctantly, Sidney began pouring drinks. After the usuals, he grunted, 'Vicar?'

'Vodka Martini, shaken not stirred,' said the vicar.

Monthi, after another nod from the vicar, went over to get them.

'Would you mind returning my hat and mask?' said Sidney, glowering at him, before whispering, fiercely, 'And where's my Pat?'.

Monthi, who had forgotten he was still wearing the hat and mask, took them off and placed them on the bar.

'Good God,' said Sir Frederick, 'It's Mike!'

'Hell's bells, Freddie, do try to keep up just a little,' said Bess.

'Sorry, Sidney,' said Monthi. 'Can we deal with other matters later, when we're not being held at gunpoint by a vicar?' He took the drinks over, including what looked like a Bloody Mary for Bess.

'Now you're probably wondering why I've called this meeting,' said Stanislav. Nobody responded. 'Sorry,' said Stanislav, 'I still have the occasional problem with the English sense of humour. Perhaps you'd like to start, Gary?'

'Certainly,' said the vicar. 'I expect you've all worked out by now that I am in fact an officer in the British security service.'

'Good lord,' said Sir Frederick. 'What a fantastic cover! Every vicar in the country an MI5 agent! Perfectly placed to pick up info, and the C of E pays their wages, not the poor bloody taxpayer!'

'Shut up, Freddie,' said Bess.

'I thought the Reverend Chassock moved on a bit hurriedly, but I put it down to the usual,' said Miss Marjoribanks. 'I underestimated you boys from over the river.'

'What on earth is the old trout talking about?' said Sir Frederick.

'Everybody but you knows Miss Marjoribanks is a retired MI6 officer,' said Bess. 'MI6 headquarters are on the south bank of the Thames, MI5 on the north bank.'

'Not retired,' said the vicar. 'That's why I'm here. We believe that she has turned rogue, and is engaged in a conspiracy to undermine our great country and the values we hold most dear.' The vicar took a small sip of his Vodka Martini. Monthi noticed that his gun hand was shaking a little.

'That's completely insane,' said Miss Marjoribanks firmly. 'Who am I supposed to be acting on behalf of?'

'I should have thought the name of your dog was a clue,' said the vicar. Putin, who was now slumbering at Miss Marjoribanks' feet, shifted a little.

'And you've ended a sentence with a preposition,' said Stanislav.

The vicar was now very pale. 'I said a conspiracy and I meant it. You are working hand in glove with our friend Mrs Demdike here to corrupt and foully pervert the pure and proud minds of the people of this country and so damage our international standing and domestic productivity.' The vicar took another sip of his Martini; his hand made Sidney's cocktail shaking superfluous. Or it would have done if Sidney had bothered.

'Oh, yes.' he continued. 'I am talking of the forces of darkness, of wild cavortings, hypnotic chanting, incessant, insinuating music, lust, desire and secret ceremonies of wild abandon!'

'Oh, come on, vicar, or whatever your name is,' said Sir Frederick. 'I think Bess might have mentioned it if she was doing all that as well as working at the post office. And anyway, what's your evidence? Have you ever seen them together? I'm blowed if I have.'

'Of course not! Do you think they would be that stupid? But I know what they're up to, oh yes. I've seen what the women of Combe Batzon are now engaged in at the Village Hall. I have studied them at length through one of the windows. I'm sure Mr Vaz, as an anthropologist, will be able to confirm their dark nature. And I've seen *The Wicker Man*. These addictive rituals are no less than a prototype of perversion that these two intend to insinuate into every village hall in the country. In no time at all quiz nights, talks with slideshows, icing/sugar flower demonstrations, visits to local tomato growing companies, gift-wrapping classes, and talks on fascinating foreign trips, with slides, will be abandoned in favour of these cultish practices that smack so clearly of the coven.'

The vicar had got his colour right back, and was sweating slightly. The emphasis placed on 'smack' together with the widened eyes had not been lost on the more alert members of the assembled company.

'Zumba,vicar,' said Monthi.

'Zumba?' said the vicar. 'Sorry, I don't speak Konkani.'

'Neither do I,' said Monthi. 'Not very well, anyway, and only when I'm in Goa. The women are doing Zumba. It's a dance and aerobic exercise practised weekly by approximately 14 million people in over 140,000 locations across more than 185 countries.'

'My God!' shouted the vicar. 'We're too late!'

'It's not really a conspiracy, and it's certainly not witchcraft,' said Monthi, exasperation overcoming self-preservation. 'I don't want to be rude, especially to a vicar with a gun, but I would have thought an MI5 agent would have known that.'

'Are you suggesting I'm not an MI5 agent?' demanded the vicar, his gun hand now wavering even more alarmingly. 'So perhaps you can also glibly explain away the disappearance of Sir Frederick's son, and Mrs Demdike's husband, and

Sidney's wife. It is my belief they had got too close to the truth, and had to be silenced.'

'I can help you with one of those,' said Monthi. 'Pat is alive. I know where she is, but I'm not at liberty to say. I was upstairs retrieving her suitcase.'

Sidney, who had started to approach Monthi from behind, was ordered by the vicar to stop.

'Put that axe down, Sidney,' said the vicar. The agitated publican complied, reluctantly.

Stanislav, judging that Miss Marjoribanks was about to say something from the determined preliminary shift of her folded arms, said quickly, 'Perhaps we could move on to Bess's husband.'

'Now that was just an unfortunate accident,' said Sir Frederick. 'Any chance of another drink, Sidney?'

'No', said Sidney.

Sir Frederick looked pained, but continued. 'Old Gordon got back from here one night and helped himself to Bess's wild garlic and coriander brew. She was up at the manor house with me of course. The old boy keeled over and karked. Bit of a fix, exposure of certain unorthodox arrangements, possible witchcraft trial, best thing to do was to bury him under the oak tree, bench on top, no one any the wiser, he'd had a good innings. Sebastian and I dug him in one rainy night after he'd been in the chest freezer for a couple of days, stiff wasn't in it. We told everyone he'd been lost at sea on a day trip to Weston-super-Mare.'

'Shut up, Freddie!' hissed Bess, her eyes flashing. For the first time, Monthi began to see her attraction. 'Still can't understand it,' she said. 'Wild garlic has been used by the followers of Hecate for centuries. We call it Devil's Garlic. Protects against other supernatural forces, including vampires and werewolves, of course, and in a paste applied correctly guarantees good health and luck, besides going rather well with coriander. I'd had a very good run with the scratch cards up till then. Silly old sod, nothing but trouble, even at the end.'

'Put it down, Sidney! I won't warn you again,' commanded the vicar as the bereft landlord once again attempted to creep up on Monthi with a sharp instrument.

'Not much of an agent, frankly,' commented Miss Marjoribanks, who would not be stilled. 'Any spook worth his licence would have drilled the patsy by now.' Sidney put the axe down very quickly.

Stanislav once again interrupted swiftly. 'Oh, dear,' he said. 'I'm afraid it's the old confusion between *colchicum autumnale and allium ursinum*.' Everyone, unsurprisingly, looked blank. '*Colchicum autumnale*,' explained Stanislav. 'The Autumn Crocus, so-called because it flowers in the autumn. But its leaves appear in the Spring, and very much resemble those of *allium ursinum*, bear's or devil's or wild garlic, which is out at the same time. But there is an important difference. The leaves of the Autumn Crocus are poisonous. There have been many cases in Slovenia. Most people survive, but it doesn't go quite as well for those with certain weaknesses, including that of the liver.'

The vicar was now looking worried as well as shaking. Monthi, slightly surprising himself as usual, addressed him. 'Come on, Gary, old lad. You've been overdoing it a bit, haven't you? All that outreach has stretched you a bit, mentally. So much easier detecting enemies of the state than soothing and saving souls, especially if you begin to get the doubts, eh?'

The vicar pulled up a chair, slumped into it, and finished off his vodka Martini in one gulp. 'Sorry, sorry, yes, that's pretty much it, really. The certainties of security versus the fallibility of faith. And I've always wanted a big gun. It's a toy, of course. Sunday's sermon lies here somewhere'.

'Don't take it too hard, vicar,' said Sir Frederick. 'We all quite like you, you know. I'll sleep through it as usual'.

Miss Marjoribanks snorted. 'Saw through you straight away. The Circus would never have a clown like you. Just a good thing I'd left the Biretta at home, or you'd have eaten lead by now.'

'Miss Marjoribanks,' said Monthi, 'You are not an MI6 officer, either, are you? Not even a retired MI6 officer. Besides your extremely shaky grasp of espionage vernacular, the Circus refers to MI6, not MI5. I've read Le Carré, you know. And I think you'll find that a *biretta* is the multi-peaked cap traditionally worn by Roman Catholic priests, not the gun manufactured by the Italian firm of Beretta. Were you by any chance an actress? I seem to remember you from an old episode of *Coronation Street*.'

'Oh, all right, I can see the game's up. How good of you to remember me. I was indeed Gladys Gaskell, late of Number 19, Coronation Street. After a distinguished career in the repertory theatre, I was going to be Albert Tatlock's love interest, but we never sparked somehow, the animal attraction wasn't there. I died when the Rover's outside cellar trap door failed unexpectedly. After that, the parts started to dry up, as they do. A good thing my late husband, Colonel Marjoribanks, left me well provided for. He was chairman of the bench in Macclesfield, which is where we met after an unfortunate misunderstanding in the Jolly Sailor on the opening night of *Hay Fever*.'

The babble of reaction that greeted this latest revelation was as suddenly stilled by the door of the Pick opening to admit Pat and Julia and a tall, handsome man Monthi didn't recognise. At the sound of his wife's voice, Sidney burst into tears. 'You've come back, Pat!' he gasped, 'You've come back! Please forgive me! I'll do anything, even smile!'

Pat was small-framed but had presence. 'I will come back, Sidney, but only on certain conditions, one of which you have already mentioned. The others are that you will do exactly as you are told and allow me to run this place without interference, and that you will refer to me by my proper name,

Pakpao, which will also be the name of this establishment from now on. We will also require a friendly and efficient barman, which could be you. And no more dressing up. Now go and run me a bath, 33 degrees centigrade, accompanying a gin and tonic with two ice cubes, and a slice of lemon, thinly cut.'

SIDNEY, AXE FORGOTTEN, rushed off to do Pakpao's bidding. The rest of the company were sitting in various states of agitation, depending on what had been disclosed about whom, except for Sir Frederick, who had gone behind the bar and was about to pour himself a glass when he was stopped dead by a look from Pakpao.

'Isn't she wonderful?' said Julia, coming over to Monthi and fixing him with those eyes. The stranger came over and took Julia's arm affectionately.

'And you,' said Monthi, increasingly confident in his newly discovered powers of detection, 'must be Sebastian. I'm very relieved to see you. There was a time when I thought you had been ritually slain to ensure a good harvest. It can be the fate of the chief's first born in certain primitive societies.'

'No! No!' said Julia, 'This isn't Sebastian, this is Roger. He's a personal assertiveness trainer, and you can tell how good he is from what he's done for Pakpao'.

'That's right,' said Roger, leaning forward rather too close to Monthi and fixing him with one of the brightest smiles he had ever seen. 'I've heard a lot about you, Matthew.'

'Actually,' said Monthi, 'It's …'

'That's right,' interrupted Roger. 'I think I can help you become more assertive, and so does Julia.'

Julia laughed, and blushed a little. Monthi couldn't decide which he liked best. 'Oh, Roger, I was only saying that Monthi…'

'That's right,' interrupted Roger. 'Julia wants me to help you with your inhibition issues.'

This, thought Monthi, was a touch rich considering he had just broken and entered a pub, jumped from a window dressed as Zorro, and solved with aplomb several enduring mysteries in under an hour. Julia laughed and blushed again; Monthi decided it was the way the pink of the blush set off the amber of the eyes.

'Oh, Roger!' she said, 'I didn't say that! I said that … '

'You said,' Roger interrupted, 'that there wasn't a second class letter's chance of arriving the next day that Matthew would break in and take Pakpao's suitcase!'

Monthi wasn't so sure about the blush now. 'Come on, Jooly baby,' said Roger, 'Let's get going to that lovenest of a hotel just outside Minehead that I've booked so we can continue where we left off last night. God, I want to feel …'

Roger was himself now interrupted by the door of the Pick, or rather, Pakpao's, being flung open by another tall, handsome man who hurled a shabby hold-all on to the floor and announced, 'Christ, Mykonos has gone off!'. Monthi, already stunned by the Roger revelations, stared while everyone else cried as one, 'Sebastian!'.

An excited gaggle formed round the Prodigal Son. Stanislav stood smiling on the edge; Monthi went over to him.

'Stan, old son,' he said. 'I've think I've had enough of Combe Batzon. All we need now is for Frank Mather and my wife to walk in on a bargain break weekend.'

'And Nigel and Dean,' said Stanislav.

The door opened again, and Hob slouched in. Bess was no longer to be seen.

'How does she do that?' said Monthi. Putin was whimpering. 'Bloody 'Ell. I'm definitely going to set up shop somewhere a little calmer. How am I supposed to finish my book with all this going on? Or mend my twice-broken heart?'

'Well, I have to confess that I was expecting more from the English village,' said Stanislav. 'That wasn't much of a murder, was it?'

'It was enough for bloody me, thank you, George Orwell. What I want is somewhere like Bolton, without the memories.'

'What about inner-city London, anonymous but not suburban. Everyone knows about the English suburbs. Terrifying body count. No, you want one of those charmingly vernacular parades of shops, shabby but useful. I might even come and open up next to you.'

Monthi brightened. 'That's not a bad idea, Stan. We could go off into the sunset to south London, like Humphrey Bogart and Claude Rains in *Casablanca.* Only for a quiet life rather than fighting for the Free French.'

'Far more chance of finding someone to help us forget, too,' said Stanislav.

'By the way, did you know that Dooley Wilson, who played Sam, couldn't play the piano? He mimed it.'

'Thanks, Stan, bloody remarkable,' said Monthi, with the happily resigned sarcasm of true affection. 'Come on, let's go.'

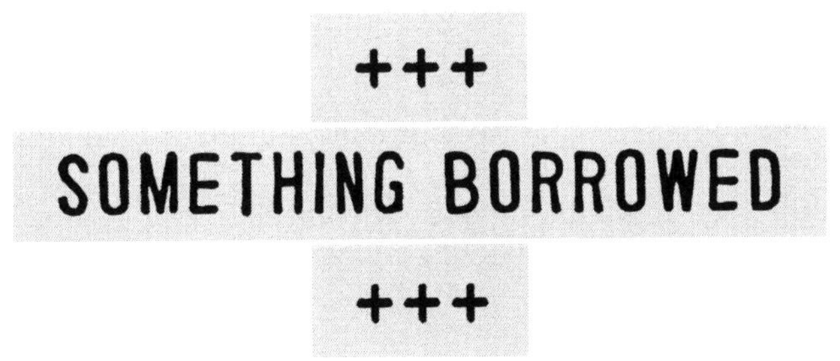
+++
SOMETHING BORROWED
+++

NEAR ANGELS +++

It had been her idea to come to Bath. He had wanted to meet nearer her home, as she would be more comfortable, more relaxed, more, good word, amenable. Perhaps a local wine bar, he had suggested, that would be the ticket. But she preferred somewhere between them. Bath would be nice. Did he know it?

He did know Bath and didn't much care for it. Everyone always seemed faintly conscious they were in Bath, on a set, to be seen. But the Georgians had taken all the rackety fun with them, and now it was just old, like most of the inhabitants. Not that he wasn't getting on himself, and rackety. His name spoke loudly of it. Clive was a believer in nominative determinism and felt his first name had removed some element of choice in his progress through life, the travelling with the samples, the coupons, the dabbling in estate agency, financial advice and fancy bathrooms – just sign here, please – and all the other innovative selling schemes, the blazers and the golf clubs where he fancied he had cut something of a dash. This was the way of the Clive. Small wonder Clive Lewis had preferred to be known as CS. And where were all the Clives now?

A seagull keened harshly and considered him without enthusiasm. They were all over Bath, brought in by the rich tip pickings, but they offended Clive's sense of place: he liked his seagulls by the sea, if at all. Actually, that would be a good name for a pub: The Incongruous Gull. Clive spent a lot of time thinking inconsequentially like this. He blamed it for his lack of success, his tendency to stray. He shifted on his bench in the square or circus or whatever it was and rubbed where his moustache had been. He had an hour before meeting June. He'd cocked the train times up, numbers were not really his thing, bit rum for a financial adviser, obviously, but there you are, and he hadn't wanted to be late. Quite a sharp breeze was blowing in from the Bristol Channel, even for November, but he didn't want to go to the cafe just yet, he financially advised himself.

June, though. A good name: a June had no airs and graces, like with a, say, Sophie, or a Caroline, but did have that bit of a twinkle lacked by a, say, Sarah, or a Susan. True, June's photograph on the Lovemedo website hadn't disclosed much of this anticipated *joie de vivre*, nor her emails; and it was also true that Clive's wife had been called Constance, and she'd left him. Still, Clive felt June had warmed a little to his bon mots and generous use of exclamation marks. And she had agreed to meet him.

Since losing Constance, there had been a succession of girls, as he was still accustomed to call them, even though none of them would see 50 again, nor, as it invariably turned out, him. Sometimes, when he was facing the future without his usual forced jauntiness, he wondered if online dating services might ever be able to come up with a life partner who would entrust her savings to a recently discharged bankrupt presently if intermittently telephoning strangers in usually vain attempts to persuade them to buy re-cycled solar panels at a special one-off price in advance while his excellent firm is in the area.

But there is something about Clive, despite the scuffed suede shoes, and the cufflinks. He is not a bad man, more a not very good one. He has made his mistakes, but, generally, he has been punished for them, as Constance would agree, if she could be found. Clive's money would be on Brighton, or Benidorm, or Margate, depending on how much is left of Clive's money, or rather the money unwisely placed by the unwise with Clive as part of his Easter Bunny Chocolate Egg Club, Royal Pets Through the Centuries mugs, Diverse Britain Celebration figurines ('From Bowler to Burqa'), the Great

Liberal Democrat Leaders set of souvenir plates, and all the rest of his imaginative but ultimately disappointing enterprises. Clive will tell you that the shortcomings of such ventures were sadly but entirely the fault of overseas suppliers, the recession, and unsympathetic and appallingly run banks punishing enterprise while at the same time paying out excessive bonuses to undeserving employees. And you will find yourself disposed to believe what Clive tells you, because Clive has convinced himself it is true, and will become quite hot under his well-worn collar about it. In more reflective mood, Clive will allow that over-enthusiasm and impetuousness might have played a small part; that and sheer bad luck. After a few more, he might also turn to thoughts of Constance, muse bitter-sweetly at her blonde memory and the cruel, inexplicable abandonment. Right now, though, Clive was thinking it was a shame he hadn't been able to persuade June to meet him in one of Bath's quite reasonably priced restaurants, Amandini's or somewhere like that, where he could have used his oh my goodness where's my wallet routine. The November dusk was drawing in; the wind had dropped, but it was still cold, the sort of day to make a man feel old and think of the thick fogs and warm fires of his youth. Clive got up, aimed a sketchy suede kick at the unimpressed gull and began to make his way to the cafe.

CONSTANCE RATHER LIKED The Victoria Art Gallery, municipal Bath's major visual arts offering. Some preferred the zappier, zeitgeistier and slightly more happening Holburne, over Pulteney Bridge and up by Sidney Gardens, but June found the Victoria's collection, with its Gainsboroughs and Lawrences, comforting. Even the Turner was a comparatively bland early water colour of the Master's. But if she wanted something more exciting there was always the prodigy Barker's

Bride of Death, pale, wan, abed and breathing her last the night before the wedding. Constance tended to follow that by going over to Herbert Henry La Thangue's merry gaggle of geese charging out of the big picture towards her, which usually cheered her up.

She had come late to Art, and was still a little defensive towards the Abstract, although some progress had been made lately with Kandinsky and Heron, and even Mondrian. In fact, Constance had come late to most of her senses. The Seventies hadn't quite been the Sixties, but she'd certainly had what they used to call a blast, involving, as far as she remembered, boutique-assisting, chalet-girling, some light hospitality and PR work, one marriage and several other failed relationships that had seemed fun at the time. By the end of the Nineties, though, she was coming to realise that there wasn't a great deal available for a blonde beginning to fade to grey generally and specifically and resorting to various bottles for both colour and cheer. A dispiriting round of demonstrating kitchen appliances and promoting packet sauces led her to the Craft and Hobby Fair at Harrogate, where she found herself on the Painting by Numbers ('Now you can be Van Gogh!') stand next to The Motorway Service Stations of Great Britain part-work stand, manned by Clive. A little older than Constance, he made her laugh and forget the dreary dwindle of the days, with his bad jokes and fine line in rueful anecdote ('So bang went another fortune!'). He rather reminded her of her father, before he left. An affair grew into an arrangement and soon and somehow they were a married couple, living in Cheltenham for some reason she had now forgotten (good for the motorway?), their time mostly spent travelling to and standing at trade fairs, part of that restless group, successors to the old commercial travellers, who tell themselves that flogging themselves and their costume jewellery, or health tonics, or pashminas, or pet baskets, or Motorway Services Stations of Great Britain part works will suddenly result in it all 'taking off' and making them rich beyond avarice, and, until it happens, you really can't beat working for yourself. So they continue to bear the irritating indifference of the punters ('Not today, thank you') and the irritating repetitious bravado of their fellow traders ('Yes, a pretty good day, all in all!') who have similarly not yet 'taken off', and never will.

Looking back, Constance couldn't quite understand, either, how she'd failed to spot how Clive had persuaded her to persevere with all this. Not all optimism is catching. But there seemed to be enough money, with the fairs supplemented by the subscriptions coming in for Clive's various enterprises, the collectable series of plates and figurines, the small savings clubs designed to finance treats, like the Easter Chocolate Bunny Club. Looking back, Constance couldn't quite understand how she'd failed to spot that the money should have been spent on Chinese factories churning out plates, figurines, chocolate bunnies, and part-works, and not on Clive and Constance. Eventually, over the very reasonable eat-all-you-can Sunday buffet at one of those expense-spared approximations of a gastro pub just outside Harrogate, Clive mentioned that 'things' were 'getting a bit tight'. He was being pursued by numbers of disappointed subscribers and the bank was being completely bloody unreasonable. 'We'll get through somehow, Connie, worry not,' he had said, taking another sip of the under-curated guest beer and raising his glass to the detached landlady, who didn't notice. Constance knew they wouldn't get through somehow; the bad news, in a place like that, so far from past chic and hopes for more, laid a cold hand on her heart. She saw nothing but trouble ahead. Still, at least he was a gent, Clive, and a bit of an old romantic: how much in love do you have to be to want a joint bank account? On the Monday, Constance transferred the little that was left; and left, too. For richer, for poorer, in sickness and in health; but, please, God, no, not for cheap buffeting every Sunday at the Fox and Hounds or other holes in corners of unambitious complacency. With a quick frown at the memory, Constance left the Victoria, paused to do up her coat and made her way past Bath Abbey in the November dusk, smiling at the famous angels, set in stone, eternally struggling up and down ladders between heaven and earth. Why didn't they fly?

CLIVE TOYED WITH HIS BUN. There was only so much pre-eating you could reasonably persuade somebody else to pay for, in his experience. Besides, his first bite had met a currant harder than *University Challenge*, and he really couldn't afford, in any sense, to lose another tooth, crown, or even, he sadly allowed to himself, a filling. This was the sort of minor, but nagging, discomfort that lack of money brought to a middle class kind of life, however rackety. A new blazer and decent haircut wouldn't go amiss, either. Then he smiled, carefully concealing the false crown that had been on 13 Top Right for seven months and for which he still owed the disturbingly young dentist £200. He had remembered one of his favourite jokes: 'Did you hear about the man who drowned in a bowl of muesli? He was pulled down by a strong currant.' Clive loved the image of a man being pulled down by a strong currant. He took another sip of tea. In one more minute, June would be late. Sometimes they didn't come at all; Clive was also quite good at spotting the ones who took a quick glance from outside and then disappeared. Nothing so far; he'd give it another ten minutes. He started to list famous dentists: Dr Crippen, Doc Holliday, the South African one who used to fizz down the wing for Leeds, Wilf Rosenberg, the Flying Dentist. The Flying Dentist! Marvellous. Thus, as ever, Clive when faced with crisis. At the Bankruptcy hearing, he'd kept calm by naming the Tottenham Hotspur 1961 double winning team to himself. When Constance left, he'd had to go through the losing Burnley side in the Spurs 1962 Cup Final triumph as well. Adam Blacklaw, for example, fine goalkeeper, but but condemned in the memory always to be sent the wrong way by the Danny Blanchflower penalty. God, he'd been an anorak as a kid, and still was. Perhaps if they'd had children. Back on that track again, bored with it, too long ago, leave it. June was promising, let's concentrate. Current favourite television programme, *Antiques Roadshow*, former favourite, the National Lottery Draw; magazines, *Country Life* and *Investors Chronicle*. Clive thought, given all this, that he could probably live with her favourite author, Jane Austen, and favourite music, *The Messiah*. A European river cruise at least seemed a certainty. Clive smiled as he always did when he remembered the delightful name of one of the operators, Viking River Cruises, picturing some particularly robust passengers arriving at swiftly abandoned destinations. It wasn't entirely clear what June did for a living; 'professional' these days covered everything from judging to footballing, and seemed most popular with what used to be called 'public servants'. But no one was a servant now, although everybody seemed to be in the services sector. Clive was having one of his blazer moments. The Polish waitress was staring at him meaningfully rather than respectfully. He smiled another careful smile and took another careful sip. It was properly dark outside now. Then Constance came in.

'CONNIE!" HE GOT TO HIS FEET clumsily, spilling the last of his tea into the saucer. 'It's you!'

She smiled broadly at him, enjoying his surprise. 'Yes, it's me. How are you, Clive?'

'I'm all right, I'm all right. Surprised to see *you*, obviously! How are you? Sit down, sit down!'

'I'm fine. A little older, naturally, and a bit wiser, hopefully.'

She did look older, Clive thought among all the other thoughts, including that he was a bit hot, which was never a good look. She had let her hair go grey, and was wearing it short. She'd put on weight, too. But she still looked nothing like the photograph.

'Well,' he said, 'this is a bit of a facer. I wasn't expecting you, of all people. You do like your surprises, Connie, don't you?' Clive beckoned the Polish waitress over while thinking back to the last surprise she had given him, rather the reverse of this one.

Constance sat down. She was feeling surprisingly composed. Clive was looking older, less carefully groomed, a little shiny at the edges, not only of his blazer. More vulnerable, she thought, with a sympathy that also surprised her. 'Yes, well, I'm sorry about that, Clive. I wasn't then, but I am now. It was just that things seemed so hopeless and you couldn't see it, you were still full of your usual maddening certainty that everything was going to be all right, whatever. It was brave, almost heroic in its way, and in my way I rather loved you for it, but I couldn't stand the life we were living any more, the mean, miserable falseness of it. I don't suppose you've changed.'

The Polish waitress delivered two cups of tea and a selection of cakes that seemed as tired as Bath. Clive patted his blazer pockets. 'You've lost your wallet,' said Constance. Clive smiled the rueful smile, the one she'd always liked. A temporary crown was in temporary touch with one of his teeth. He needed a haircut; what had been tousled was now wispy.

'Sorry, darling,' he said, 'Just reflex.'

'Like the "darling",' said Constance.

Clive looked surprised. 'That's right, that's right.' He did some more distracted patting. 'Actually, you're not going to believe this, but I really have lost my wallet.' They both laughed, and found it comfortable. 'Not that there was anything much in it,' he said. 'You did rather clean me out, you know,' he added, giving her his old recriminating look, the one where his head went down and he looked out mournfully from under his eyebrows. 'Where did you go? Was it Benidorm? Barbados?' He gave her his rueful smile again.

'Do me a favour, Clive. I've got a little more class than that. Besides, how much do you think was in the account? There was barely enough to get to Bridlington.'

'What did you do, then? Did you invest our money wisely? Or win the lottery?'

'Both, actually. I bought a Lotto ticket with it, and won £20,000. I got a job in an antiques shop. I'm pretty good at selling if you remember, especially when I'm interested, and it's not chocolate bunnies or motorway service station part-works.'

Clive winced. 'We were just unlucky there. The time wasn't quite right. We could have done it. People are fascinated by service stations. I know a man who can recite the M6 ones, both ways, and then there's Chigwell, on the the M11, which has never been built, and Happendon, great name, on the M74, you can get haggis there, you know …' He broke off, recognising Connie's smile, and finding again how much he loved it, how much he would love it to go on full beam, crinkles and dimples and bright eyes in top beguilement. 'Sorry, I was forgetting you've heard all this before. Ok, the ideas were crap. Not much better since, to be honest, either. Unless you fancy some solar panels. We are in your area.'

The jokes were still there, and the brittle brightness, but this Clive was a frayed, afraid Clive. Constance's sudden, unexpected appearance had cracked the customary front, the cheerful confidence that was his security, his protection against the truth, whether about his failures, or his doubts, or the need to be loved, and not to be left, even or especially if you are turned 60, overweight, and pretty broke. And especially not to be left, he realised, by Connie, who had almost smiled at the solar panel sally. He had prepared lots of carefully insouciant stuff for this meeting, if it ever happened – 'I'm sorry about Harrogate, Clive'; 'Ah, yes, Harrogate, I remember it well. You were in blue, the bathroom suite was beige'. But his nursed hurt had melted away before the reality of her, and with the realisation that he had, in fact, been a silly old fool. He wanted to tell her he still loved her, would always love her, could they start again, he'd be sensible this time, wouldn't touch the Lotto money, no, couldn't think what had made him think of that. Instead, he said: 'I see there's a performance of *The Messiah* at the Abbey next week. Fancy it?'

'I'd love to,' said Constance. 'I've taken up singing in a choir. We did *The Messiah* last year. Such fantastically infinite, transcending, moving music, and so good for letting and getting everything out. It helps me relax, and sometimes I really need that. But you were never into choral singing before, Clive. Those sailors singing *There Is Nothing Like A Dame* in *South Pacific* was about as far as you went in that direction.'

'You never used words like "transcending" before. Isn't that something to do with sex? Sorry, a bit feeble, best I could manage at short notice. To be honest, I found there was only so much consolation you could get from Rodgers and Hammerstein, and *'You'll Never Walk Alone'* didn't quite cut it, given the circumstances. I've missed you, Connie.'

Clive had to work hard to resist saying, 'I'd grown accustomed to your face', even though it was Lerner and Loewe and one of the worst things he could have said. He had this compulsion to lighten conversations, try jokes, especially bad ones, because it was much easier than revealing that he was hurt and afraid and lonely and frightened that she might laugh at silly old Clive.

'You have changed, Clive, haven't you? Before, you wouldn't have been able to say you missed me without rushing to add something silly like "I'd grown accustomed to your face", because you couldn't stand being honest and leaving yourself open to the slightest possibility of rejection. You always had to have your comedy escape clause.'

She'd changed, too, Clive told himself as she looked across at him with the old smile. He took refuge behind his cup and a Bourbon biscuit that was just on the turn from crunch to crumple. More confident, certainly more intelligent than he remembered; his blonde assumptions had probably got in the way, then, and his need to be in charge, not to be threatened. And he certainly wasn't the brightest spoon in the tea shop himself, as Life had tended to prove, a mind wasted on trivia, frightened of the bigger things, like love.

Constance busied herself in turn with the tea pot and a fig roll that could look the Bourbon biscuit right in the eye in terms of peerage. This was pretty stupid, she told herself, even if it had seemed a good idea at the time. Clive was the past, the insecure past, the charade, the brassy self-deceit, before the silence when the hubbub dies and you're left with just yourself. She was more honest with herself now, more comfortable. She'd started taking notice, opening up, the art, the antiques, the singing, the interested attendance at small arts and book festivals. She'd not long been back from an educational cruise to the Black Sea, guest lecturers and bracing excursions. Clive was at best a river cruise man, large lunches and yellow pullovers up the Rhine, the exciting annual break from the golf club. Still, he had volunteered *The Messiah*. And he was Clive. How many people do you meet in your life that you feel easy with, really easy, effortlessly easy? In her case, Clive. And so what if the luck of that draw gives you someone less than Samson-like, someone who's feckless, frivolous, but essentially and unfashionably kind of heart? The sex hadn't been great, admittedly, but there had been a fine and cuddly quality to it, and she had never given up entirely on coaxing Clive into something more lively. He was now telling her a joke about a man being drowned in muesli and her laughter was partly at herself for getting so ahead of herself: sex! Clive was looking across at her, delighted at her laughter, his face winningly open and affectionate. She thought of the lyrics from *My Funny Valentine*, Rodgers with the great Hart this time, the one which like so many others Clive played too often, with Ella Fitzgerald as usual exactly between plaintive and piquant; the one where the fallible flawed flabby hero of the title still manages to make his lover smile with her heart. Smile with her heart! Clive!

CONNIE WAS GIVING him that full crinkle of a smile. He began to doubt his luck on this cold, grey November day. 'Blimey, I've missed that laugh, Connie!' he said. What other joke could he tell her? He didn't have many new ones. Perhaps this was the moment to be brave and tell her how much he loved her and how lonely he had been without her and could they please try again. After all, she must want that, too, or she wouldn't have gone to all this trouble finding him, so how risky could it be? Clive, new Clive, took the plunge. 'Connie, would you like to…' In the way of these things, this was the moment the Polish waitress chose to inquire, with even less than the usual sincerity, 'Is everything all right for you?'. 'More tea, Connie?,' Clive continued. 'Yes, please,' said Constance. 'Cake?' Connie looked over at the slightly collapsed half of chocolate gateau in pride of place on the counter. 'No, thank you,' she said. The waitress, inscrutable, went off. They looked at each other in the silence that always follows. 'Is this a seventies tribute cafe you've chosen, Clive?' she said. 'What next, fondue?'

Clive gave one of his happy sniggers. He'd forgotten how much he liked being teased by Connie. 'This is really amazing,' he said. 'I can't believe it. I know this sounds terribly old hat, but I hadn't realised how much I missed you. I've been lonely, really lonely since you left, Connie, but it isn't just that. I've tried to find someone else, but it hasn't worked. The ones who clearly thought I was a silly, rather pathetic specimen, with the jokes and the blazer, were only marginally outnumbered by the ones who obviously thought I was principally interested in their money. True in both cases, I suppose. But you know the jokes and the blazer are just the sad armour I wear to face the world, to get by. Hark to me, though: "sad armour". I'm not much of a knight, am I? Hardly once a night, if you remember. But I'm only the real me when I'm with you, Connie, and I like the real me more than the knight me, and I want to drop all the crap and bluster, and be with you. Connie …'

With repeated impeccable timing, the waitress arrived with the tea, sans gateau. For once in his overly aware life, Clive took no notice. 'I love you, Connie, will you come back to me?' The waitress paused, waiting. Connie looked at him with the sweetest smile, wrinkles and dimples in perfect combination, the smile which told Clive that, wonderfully, everything was going to be fine, at last. 'Yes, Clive, I will. And by all means lose the blazer, but keep the jokes.' Now they were both smiling at each other, with the complete lack of reserve, inhibition, distraction and qualification that only those who love know but the less fortunate can see when loved photographs lover. 'So, everything is all right for you,' said the waitress.

JUNE TURNED AWAY from the teashop. She'd only been five minutes late, but there was no one there remotely resembling Clive's photograph (she had fancied he bore a bit of a likeness to Cary Grant in *North By Northwest*). It wasn't the first time she'd been stood up; this, though felt particularly bitter and hopeless, on a dank day heading grimly towards a lonely Christmas, with no one to plan a future with over the sherry: the River cruises, the nice meals out, and what to do with the surprising amount of money Ron's untimely death (struck down on the 17th by a rogue ball from the 3rd) had brought to her. But it was more than that; more than the hard dark November cold; more than the fuss, the anticipation, the waste of a good hair-do: no, it was the sight of that pair in the teashop, oblivious to everything including their ordinariness, such was their luminous delight in each other. June walked back to the station, alone, through a Bath that had seen it all before, and didn't care.

In a Bath Teashop
By John Betjeman

'Let us not speak, for the love we bear one another --
Let us hold hands and look.'
She, such a very ordinary little woman;
He, such a thumping crook;
But both, for a moment, little lower than the angels
In the teashop's ingle-nook.

TOUR DE FORCE +++

Looking back – and I've had plenty of time to think about it – the most enjoyable moment for me was when Harry dropped his trousers. It hadn't been a restrained gathering before that, but the revelation of Harry's (perfectly respectable) polkadot boxers signalled a change from general jollity into one of those dizzy passages of deliciously liberating mayhem and misrule and escape from tedious old strait-laced civilisation that seems to be required from time to time, especially if you're male, and English. You will appreciate it even more when I tell you that Harry was then a middle-aged solicitor. And that there had been absolutely no hint of what was to follow when he rose to respond on our behalf to the generous and graceful remarks of the chief of our hosts.

Harry was wearing a blazer and tie as well as the trousers. His French was confident and beyond reproach for sounding anything else but English. His sentiments were grave, unimpeachable: '*Merci, mes amis …cette repas magnifique … votre hospitalité vraiment extraordinaire …*'. It is true that he had climbed on to the long trestle table in front of him, better, we thought, to be seen and heard. And, although it was pretty noisy, he had commanded attention. But then, suddenly, he equally gravely and deliberately unbuckled his belt, unbuttoned his trousers, and did it. Why, he couldn't explain afterwards, falling back on that well-known and all-encompassing justification beloved of politicians: 'It seemed the right thing to do'.

Anyway, thereafter my memory is of increased noise, laughter, shouting, singing, several Harry imitators and a Conga of mighty proportions working its way round the room. The French seemed pretty good at the mayhem thing, too. I didn't know they were familiar with the Conga, let alone *Do You Know*

The Muffin Man?, where competitors singing the old Victorian song attempt to negotiate obstacles, chairs, tables, and kneeling comrades while balancing glasses of beer on their heads after the style of the old street sellers. It was very popular with British officers in the Second World War, another, rather larger, incidence of male chaos. And we were, of course, an all-male gathering, apart, obviously, from Jan, but, if I remember rightly, which is not guaranteed, she was the only Muffin person to get through the course without spilling a drop.

Well, yes, I know, this sort of thing isn't everyone's, how should I say, *tasse de thé*. I recall, even longer ago, a sassy sort of (American) West Coast woman commenting on an evening of loud conviviality involving drink and men hugely amused by themselves and each other: 'Male bonding. Heavy.' It also involved rugby, a pursuit rarely discussed where aesthetes gather. A suspicion of a fatal lack of sensitivity when compared to, say, cricket, which is conceived to be delivering an important cultural message by virtue of its stately impenetrability. Poets have paeaned and played cricket. Becket, for Godot's sake, actually played first class cricket. And sport surely has no lovelier line than in Francis Thompson's *At Lords,* 'As the run-stealers flicker to and fro'. Even football has contrived to become 'the beautiful game' and to attract intellectual analysis and philosophical approval (although I believe this owes rather too much to the proximity of Arsenal to the leafier reaches of North London, and to their longstanding coach, a Frenchman with an accent that bestows gravity upon the most banal of utterances, despite its similarity to that of the Surete's non-pareil, Jacques Clouseau). But rugby? The last recorded sensitive soul was a Harlequins scrum-half called Jeremy in the Sixties who abandoned his England career and the game to go off basket-weaving in Provence. (I should point out that I'm talking about Rugby Union, not the other code, Rugby League, one of the North's greatest gifts to the world, a game of fiercely concentrated force and flair not to be trifled with by the likes of us.)

But to return to the trousers. Why were we there? Well, rugby players can ponder deeply, too, especially the morning after. But, in the most immediate sense, we were on a bit of what we used to call 'a jolly', that formalised and generally more harmless re-creation of the war party known as the sporting tour. True, anyone observing us, Peter, Davey, Dan, Harry and all, would have noted that we were a little old for it.

And age was the thing, really. For some, you will have noticed, the flight of time's arrow prompts ambitions untempered by realism. It would still have been a challenging trip had we been ten years younger; but an ancient imperative was in operation. Although the anxieties of women approaching 40 tend to attract more attention, there is for men of the same age an inkling growing into a conviction that the quality which used to lend us much of our point is fading faster than a horse tipped by an Irish priest after a good lunch at Cheltenham.

And it bothers us. To the male, the condition of his physique remains a potent pointer despite or perhaps because of the diminishing reliance placed upon it in these supposedly sophisticated times. In his late thirties, he begins to feel the toll of the years after a concentrated period of hunting and gathering: possibly the four plastic supermarket bags in each hand seem to be weighing more heavily than they did; perhaps the eye for the parking space is not what it was. A bleak future beckons, where sitting down is never unaccompanied by a sigh, where the easy lope across the busy road is replaced by the determinedly dignified fast walk, where the meditative pause between socks gets longer and longer, and beige is worn. The hot breath of youth is at his back and the way ahead is steep and difficult for what he will all too soon be calling his 'pins'.

Some will get a motorbike, or a new wife. We went on tour, an ageing Sunday rugby side, feeling all of the above, unfit for the purpose but enthusiastic; nursing fading dreams and unrealistic estimations of skills that had been cruelly robbed of expression by a conspiracy of fate and other factors like a disinclination to train on cold winter nights or the inability to run very quickly. And when Peter suggested it, in a cold November for the following Spring, distance lent expectation untroubled by practicality or those increasing aches in the places where, to adapt Leonard Cohen slightly, we played.

Peter was a tall, thin man who imagined himself a rangy back row forward, as mean as he was in fact mild. But he was also one of those people without whom amateur sport would not exist, an organiser, a volunteer. Why do they do it, these secretaries, linesmen, referees, coaches? Altruism, fellow feeling, insecurity, need to control, or all of it? No matter, they are to be cherished, as was the sight of Peter before every game, in the car park of wherever we were playing, hopping from one leg to the other, craning in hope of our arrival. He had found this chap – another of his sainted kind – who operated a sort of clearing service for junior clubs keen to do a bit of foreign touring.

'He's got lots of French clubs who are dead nuts keen on playing English teams,' said Peter in the clubhouse after a fairly narrow defeat against The Highwaymen. This stirring name belied their rather more down-to-earth employer, The Road Research Laboratory. But we were holding back on our usual highly amusing references to daylight robbery, as they had lent us one of their players when Peter's increasingly agitated wait for Bill had not been rewarded. But that was Bill. And the Highwayman had, inconveniently, scored all our points.

'The French team will put us up in their homes, so that helps with the cost,' said Peter. 'The major expense will be transport. But just think of it, good weather round Easter, fine wines, good food and not too challenging opponents brimming with *entente cordiale*. It'll be terrific. Thanks, Charlie, just a half, thank you.'

I went off to get Peter his drink (and one for myself) while various team members reacted to the tour plan in fairly typical ways. Dan, our fly-half, was keen. The fly half is the artist of the rugby team. He is at a remove from the sweat and grunting of the forwards; he is the play maker, the creative player who provides the telling pass, the shrewd kick and the swift dart that breaks through the opposing defence. I have rarely come across a fly-half who didn't check himself in the changing room mirror before running out, and Dan was certainly no exception to that, or to a supreme belief in his abilities, boosted in this case by his constant reminder that he had played for the legendary Neath Grammar School, considered at one time as a bit of a 'conveyor belt' in the matter of fly-halves, and Welsh ones at that. It was Dan's view that a trip to France at Easter would be just the ticket, especially as the firmer, less muddy pitches over there at that time of the year would really suit the playing style of an elusive runner like himself. 'Happy days,' he said, before ordering a Pernod.

The fly-half is served by the scrum-half, the no-nonsense link between forwards and backs, with a bit of both and a bit of mongrel, as we rugby players term a feisty, spirited player. This was especially true in our case, as our scrum-half, Jan, was a woman. We didn't make much of this, as, strictly speaking, mixed rugby is not allowed beyond the age of 15 out of concern for the superior physicality of the male. Jan, though, was pretty tough, but not in an aggressively butch way: you should imagine a slightly stockier version of Gwyneth Paltrow's boy character in *Shakespeare in Love*. Certainly she was far better able to look after herself than I was; despite my large size, I often remind myself of Paul Gallico's self-description as he prepared to box the mighty Jack Dempsey for a magazine article: 'Inside this giant beat the heart of a rabbit'. As for orientation, we were mostly concerned about her movement on the pitch, which was at least as good as any of the rest of us.

People who know little of rugby and its culture often point out the large amount of close physical contact, arms around each other, cheek against cheek and cheek against thigh in the scrum, the wrestling in the mud, and so forth; in my experience, though, anything of that sort is buried deep in the unconscious, something which rugby players are not generally in touch with unless there has been a collision of some sort. Anyway, Jan was very keen, too. 'Sounds fun,' she said. 'Will you boys all be at the back of the coach singing rude songs while I get on with some knitting or do torrid things to the driver that don't involve him taking his eyes off the road?'

'Well,' said Harry, with that air of addressing the bench in mitigation of a TS10 (Traffic Light Signals, Failure to Comply) offence which never entirely leaves a certain sort of solicitor, 'That would be traditional. As would be, I suggest, a crate of brown ale, and waving out of the back window. Marvellous. I should make it clear, though, that when I refer to traditional activities on a motor coach engaged on hire, I do not include certain activities being conducted with the driver of a torrid nature, whether distracting or not'. Harry then giggled winningly at his sally. With friends and team mates, affection and enjoyment is a lot to do with recognition and repetition of their tics and trademarks, I find.

Bill seemed keen, too, when he finally pitched up. 'Terribly sorry, Pete. Overslept. Bit of a rough night last night, too many pints at the Harrow, then on for an Indian, then I lost the door key, you know how it is.'

'But that's how it was last time, Bill,' said Peter. 'How many keys have you lost?' Bill smiled the same rueful smile he smiled whenever he dropped the ball, which was fairly often. Most teams of our kind tended to have a highly unreliable but infectiously enthusiastic member: they're usually pushed out to play on the wing, which was where Bill played. 'My replacement sounds pretty good, though,' said Bill brightly. 'Anyone got a fag?'.

The drinkers exchanged smiling glances: that was Bill, who was immediately enthusiastic about the tour, although more smiles, allied this time with raised eyebrows, were exchanged when he muttered something about his passport.

Davey, though, could be relied on to spoil any happy consensus, being a northerner. Or more properly, one of those northerners for whom a day is not satisfactorily passed without entering at least five deflating caveats to any plan, hope or dream; in short, a Yorkshireman. Davey was our full-back; his first name was actually Peter, but that had got him confused with the other Peter, so Davey he was, although I sensed that he felt calling him by his surname was some sort of upstairs-downstairs, north-south slight. But it was easy to slight Davey; I sometimes wonder how many slights make a chip.

It certainly wouldn't do to mention that Davey played Union rather than League because he'd been to a posher school. Besides, he was our best player, which we never mentioned, either, as he already knew. Davey wasn't in the mould of today's attack-loving full backs who can transform defence into attack in an instant with a shimmy or change of pace; rather more importantly, given the players in front of him, he was a dour, rock-solid last line of defence with a formidable clearing kick.

Did I say dour? 'You won't get the numbers,' he said. 'And then no one will pay up in time. And they'll be some top team who'll give us a right thrashing. Why don't we fix up something with Normanton's sixth team, they'd go easy on us if I had a word. Not sure if they'd offer us any beds, though. No thanks, I'll buy me own.' This last was in response to my usual offer to buy him a drink because I enjoyed the reply, which was always the same.

But you'll be wondering about what sort of jobs were undertaken by our gallant XV. Harry, you know about. Peter was a sub-editor on the local newspaper, a job requiring method, accuracy, patience, and, in Peter's case, punctiliousness bordering on pedantry. I knew this because I was a reporter on the paper, specialising in reporting on the local council and nostalgia. No one was quite sure what Bill did. Dan was in marketing and Davey was a ladies hairdresser. No one was quite sure how good he was, as Jan refused to go to him. 'Can you imagine his small talk?' she used to say. None of the various girl friends, wives and partners did, either. Actually, none of them came to our games, apart from the occasional visit early in a relationship, rarely repeated. Rugby of the Union kind can be pretty dull even when practised by the top professional players, which we weren't.

Jan was a Pilates instructor. No one was quite sure how good she was, either, as no self-respecting junior casual rugby player of our type would risk anything quite so, how would you say, non-contact. These were the team stalwarts, supported by a changing cast of friends and friends of friends who would play for a little then drift away as jobs elsewhere or family demands or a growing realisation of how bad we were kicked in. There were usually an Australian or a New Zealander or two passing through; at present, unusually, we had an American, Al, whose shaky grasp of the game was compensated, sometimes, by his great size and the vicarious coolness we felt a black New Yorker lent us, even though his Ivy League education and current position as an investment banker appeared to have removed his rap gene. No Kanye he. Nor should we forget Tom, a retired accountant who had adopted us. He was our chairman and invariably only supporter, a genial man who knew even less than Al about the game, showed not the slightest interest in learning any more but enjoyed a bit of fresh air on the touchline and a few drinks in the bar afterwards.

The season progressed as our seasons did: a few wins, a few embarrassing defeats, and one glorious victory against the Old Berkhamians, a loud and lofty outfit who usually loudly and loftily clobbered us. Dan was unavailable, and the Old Berks exchanged meaningful glances as Neil, the replacement fly-half, stubbed his cigarette out by the touchline before shambling on in borrowed kit, coughing. He had not checked in the mirror. We won the first scrum, Jan whipped it back to Neil, and he banged a drop goal over from fully 40 yards (we continued to spurn the newfangled metric business). Open-mouthed doesn't begin to describe the Berks. Why can't real life be like that? Why, to take the smallest example, does the driver who refuses to let you out never present an opportunity to do exactly the same to him (and it always is a him) shortly afterwards? I told you rugby lends itself to philosophical thinking. And, just occasionally, deep joy, as Neil orchestrated a seemingly effortless victory. Even I scored, from fully five yards. Neil never played for us again. Indeed, no one ever saw him again, or remembers who brought him along. But this is the way it is with this sort of rugby: they come and they go. Some of them might even be ghosts of former greats, keeping their hand in. Certainly no one laid one on him that day. Do you remember Wilson the Wonder Athlete, prodigious at any game, and alive since 1795 after receiving the gift of eternal life from a convenient hermit? No? He was in the *Hotspur* comic and really good. Rugby players of our type tend to remember this sort of thing. But I used to keep these more fanciful thoughts to myself.

PETER GAVE US various updates about the tour as it grew nearer. We now knew where we were going: a small town south of Paris, Videcoume. 'Nestling in the French *campagne*,' said Peter, who was romantic as well as pedantic. 'Just the one game, Saturday afternoon, plenty of time to get back on Sunday. Leave on Friday, bit of *Oh là là* in Paris that night, staying at a modest *pension* arranged by my new best friend, Pierre, their captain. They'll host a dinner on the Saturday night, and he's already sorted out beds for us there. I must say he's a bit of a stickler for detail, almost overboard with it.' Dan and I exchanged meaningful glances taking in the clipboard Peter had taken to carrying about with him.

'What sort of standard will these teams be?' asked Davey, wary as ever.

'Mixed ability, he says, nothing too challenging.'

'You could say the same about England,' said Dan, in that Welsh way.

'Well, there's no point in worrying about it,' said Peter. 'We've faced some tough encounters in the past and acquitted ourselves pretty well.' I thought it prudent not to mention the Old Mastodonians, two weeks before.

'Very Henry V,' said Davey.

'That's one of our kings, Al,' said Jan,

'Ah, yes,' said Al. '1387-1422. Died on his third French tour from a toxic megacolon, unless I'm a mistaken ignorant black merchant banker homie'. You see what I mean about Al.

The main problem was transport. No problem with the ferries, but the principal mode was proving difficult. We needed something capable of taking around 20 people, 15 with a few players over to cover various contingencies, injuries, lost, overslept, hung over, deserted, that sort of thing. Plus our travelling support, of course: Tom was very keen to come. But the right size of coach at the right cost was proving tricky.

It was Tom who came up with the answer. He had, apparently, a friend, also called Tom, who owned a garage near him, and was a bit of a jackdaw where transport was concerned. 'Tom's got some amazing stuff,' said Tom. 'Classic cars, personnel carriers, vintage tractors, road rollers, low loaders, one half of a Harrier jump jet, Sinclair C5, you name it. And he has just taken possession of something rather special which he thinks might do us. Do you remember Too Late The Tourniquet?'

Harry was immediately excited. 'Too Late The Tourniquet? The finest exponents of slash rock heavy metal ever to thrash out a diminished fifth while flicking sweat off split ends and black leather into head-bobbing computer enthusiasts? The world's been a poorer place since they left the stage. Zak is now a motivational speaker, Rik has his own chain of budget boutique hotels, Jimi is an ordained minister and Tag has his own chutney label. What about them?'

The rest of us were looking at Harry with some awe. We were used to his impressive and eclectic collection of minor obsessions, but not this one, which was considerably more edgy and *outré* than, say, his almost photographic recollection of the works of Britain's leading matchstick hobbyists. Tom seemed less impressed, but then he did know a man who collected jump jets. 'Well,' he said, 'they had this fabulous bijou coach they used to tour in, all rock cons. It's a touch worse for wear, obviously, rock stars, you know, but he says we can borrow it before he starts to restore it.'

'Fantastic,' said Harry. 'I'll bring some Tourniquet tracks along. You'll love *Entrail Blues* and *Get My Kicks From 666*'.

'Only if I can bring my Sinatra collection,' said Dan. I mentioned that professional players these days seemed to listen to their own music through headphones. Al mentioned Vera Lynn, but I think he was joking.

WE ASSEMBLED EARLY on the Friday morning at Tom's house. He was waiting outside. No one had ever been inside. A Mrs Tom had been mentioned, only occasionally, but there was no sign of life within. In any case, our attention was very much taken by the coach, which Tom had picked up from the other Tom the night before. It was white, very white, where the bodywork was not covered by some striking and large customised illustrations, including several headless corpses lying in pools of blood, four lively figures identified by

Harry as Zak, Rik, Jimi and Tag snarling and hurling vigorous vee signs at the world over the shoulders of a succession of caressing sirens, mostly in leather, some free adaptations of the more doom-laden works of Hieronymus Bosch, and a liberal scattering of musical notes, motorbikes, assault rifles and skulls. The doorway was straddled by another large siren, beckoning entry in a more than friendly fashion.

'Bloody Hell!' said Dan.

'Pretty much par for the course for the boys,' said Harry.

'Bloody amateurs,' said Davey. 'They've got the trigger guard on the Kalashnikov completely wrong.'

'I am not travelling on that thing,' said Jan. Faces fell. Not only was Jan a good scrum half, but if she didn't come it would mean Peter playing there instead. Peter was already very bossy on the field, and playing in this key position would allow him to be even more so. He was also a terrible scrum half. And Jan was fun.

She saw our distress, and relented. 'All right, all right. But I'm only boarding on the understanding that my presence is ironic, knowing, post-modern and in no way an endorsement of the sexist crap emblazoned all over this bus. In addition, I shall be wearing dark glasses both on embarking and alighting.' The rest of us applauded as she embarked, indeed wearing dark glasses.

We were in any case sympathetic. Rugby players are more socially liberal than is generally allowed, certainly when compared to footballers, for whom being caught in the possession of The Guardian is enough to cause grave worry and can lead to ostracism or worse.

Harry began to explain to Jan at length that one of the Tourniquets' top tracks, *'Stop Bitchin', You in the Kitchen'*, was in fact a self-lacerating admission of male inadequacy. Jan was only half listening, the rest of her attention taken, understandably, by the interior decor, which was striking. White leather seats alternated with crimson ones; every second row was interrupted by banquettes shaped like lips (crimson, naturally) or rolls of bandage (yup, white). The back of the coach was taken up by a piano which on closer inspection, by Dan, turned out to be a giant cocktail cabinet, empty but for a half-eaten cocktail sausage, stick still intact. Most of the seats had large rips in them and swathes of ceiling hung down at random intervals. It was as if a mad knifeman had been let loose, or possibly two. A mannequin lay splayed across one of the luggage racks, a traffic cone on another.

'Welcome,' said the driver. 'Cool or what?'

'Or what,' said Davey, whose humour was obviously not improved by an early start, despite his proud industrial heritage.

'I'm Pierce,' said the driver. 'Former Tourniquets roadie and occasional sidesman when Zak was indisposed. Or Jimi. Tag crashed out a few times, too. And Rik, come to think of it. We lived, man, we lived. But all things must pass, as George H said. I was a racing driver, once. Only Formula Two, mind. But the boys liked to go at a bit of a lick'.

Pierce's grey hair was best Seventies rock drummer, long at the back and short at the front. His face looked lived in, and slept in. Harry gestured towards the slashes and swathes. ' Yeah, right,' said Pierce. 'That was after a bad gig in Rhyl. Have you been to Rhyl in February? Or maybe it was Mold. Anyway, it was a mistake to come on board and ask for Rik's autograph and then say, "Thanks, Ozzie". Tom's not sure whether to leave it like this in tribute, or clean it up a bit. Personally, I like it like this. All of these stains have a story to tell. Everyone here? Early for you, is it? Different for me, I haven't been to bed yet.'

We were indeed all there, Jan, Peter, Davey, Dan, Harry, assorted other stalwarts and less stalwarts, me, Tom, and Al. But Bill wasn't, obviously. His phone was switched off, or, more likely, somewhere else. Peter gave him another five minutes, and then Pierce, who had by now donned Aviators, driving gloves and earphones, set off at a surprisingly sedate pace. The case of brown ale had been brought on with bravado and placed in the piano, but it was ignored. There was in the coach that fuzzy silence that follows an unaccustomed dawn, except for Harry, obviously, who was now discussing in some depth the Tourniquets' seminal second album, *Rip Away The Drip*.

By the time he had reached the sixth album, *Handsaw Screams*, quite a lot had happened. Jan had long since moved away, explaining she needed to get some sleep. Harry had taken to moving round the coach and giving his Tourniquet thoughts to anyone available, currently Peter, who seemed to be taking notes. The ferry crossing had gone reasonably well. We'd left Pierce in the headphones with hands still on the wheel, and, possibly, asleep: it was difficult to tell with the Aviators. There were some strange looks at the coach and us from our fellow passengers, as you might expect, but I for one rather enjoyed being taken for an edgy unleasher of hell, and Harry rather enjoyed talking Tourniquet to anyone who would listen. Davey wasn't so keen, but I think he would have been upset to be mistaken for anyone who wasn't from Yorkshire. And, in any case, heavy metal and hairdressers are not a natural fit. Tom was becoming ever more amiable with each passing bottle of brown ale. Peter was trying without success to contact Bill from the top of the ship, where Jan was doing a quick Pilates work-out, much to Dan's disdain. 'You don't want to leave it in the gym,' he said, taking another sip of Pernod. Al was immersed in his lap top, banking. Everybody happy, then, in their own way.

There was a short delay at Customs: you couldn't expect any *douanier* worth his *Canal Rouge* to ignore a coach such as ours. But Harry's French and demeanour passed it off very well, particularly as they seemed in a hurry not to hear any more about Tourniquet's concept album, *And Out Through The Nose*, or *Exit Par Le Nez*, as he put it. It helped, too, I think, that we had persuaded Pierce to remove the headphones and Aviators.

The trip to Paris was uneventful, once we had got him clear about driving on the right: 'Hamburg, Strasbourg, Amsterdam, Reeperbahn, remember, Pierce, the old days?' Peter, with the help of Pierre, had found us an unexceptionable *pension* which would have benefited from being a little less in the shadow of *La Santé* prison; still, as Harry pointed out, our coach was unlikely to be stolen. The night in Paris passed much as you might expect of a rugby tour: before finding a restaurant for a civilised meal, a quick bar stop for what Dan termed a 'heart-starter' which became ever-extended and ever more exuberant before M Le Patron suggested a termination and gaggles of genial, gently swaying Anglais peeled off to find a pizza or bed muttering 'big day tomorrow, Monsieur', *haute cuisine* untroubled. Except for Tom, of course, who, finally defeated by brown ale, hadn't made it out of the *pension*; and Dan, who disappeared in the opposite direction and had to be let in at three am by Peter, who was still trying to contact Bill, without success. We'd also lost a couple of Australians, but that was par for the course.

THE NEXT MORNING, only a certain pallor and uncertain grasp on coffee cups betrayed the night before. Dan answered all inquiries with the significant winking that generally signals a lack of it. We found Pierce still as rigid in the driver's seat as we'd left him; masterly map-reading by Al translated for Pierce by the odd interpolation of 'Man', and 'Hang' as in 'Hang a left here' saw us arrive at the Videcoume club house well before lunch.

Peter instructed Pierce to park round the corner, so as not to disturb our hosts too much. Pierre was waiting for us outside the clubhouse, carrying a clipboard. The clubhouse was a fine construction in the familiar concrete that is Le Corbusier's most striking gift to all parts of France. Still, I wasn't going to get too sniffy, as our humble side could only cadge the use of a clubhouse back home. It also prompted Davey to mutter about the home side's clearly superior credentials and the gloomy certainty that we were in for 'a right tonking'.

Inside we were introduced to the other team members who would be putting us up, and then invited to sit down to a light *repas* of some rather fine *hors d'oeuvres* with a red wine that Tom described as 'most acceptable'. The rest of us, warned by a glance from Peter, stuck to the fizzy water. Even Dan seemed to be getting into what he call 'the zone', evidenced by an abstinence from the Pernod and several rather long anecdotes designed to demonstrate the superiority of Welsh rugby, only partly understood by our hosts, who nevertheless nodded at every mention of 'Barry John' and 'Phil Bennett', two legendary fly halves with whom Dan saw himself sharing peerage. There was obviously some confusion about whether Dan had played with them, and that he must have been very young, but I judged this would do us no harm come the game.

There was also a slight *frisson* when Harry asked his neighbour to pass the 'Vichy Water', setting Tom off on a disquisition that I could see might develop unhelpfully, and which I managed to head off by asking him if this was his first time in France. Tom allowed that it was, but said he had long been an admirer of Petula Clark. Our hosts again looked rather puzzled, as did Tom when Jan quietly congratulated him on his 'mind games'. 'I don't remember that one,' he said. 'Was it the B side of *Downtown*?'

It was at this point that Bill entered, looking even more *distrait* than usual. 'Hello everyone!' he said, brightly. 'Sorry, Peter. Overslept.'

Peter presented his usual mixture of affront and relief: 'We'd really given you up this time, mate. I'm getting too old for this, I so am. How did you manage it?'. Bill had hitched a ride with his old biker mate, Stew, who, luckily, had fancied a weekend break. 'I've never ridden pillion before for any length of time, interesting. He's with your bloke, now, the one in the Aviators who looks asleep, but isn't. Mmm, food. *Bonjour*, everybody'. Bill sat down and started eating steadily, eyes firmly on his plate.

'We're kicking off in half an hour, Bill,' remonstrated Peter, further and familiarly agitated.

'Don't worry, Pete, I've got terrific metabolism. Have you heard of Cockney Cliff Watson? Played rugby league for St Helens and Great Britain. Always had a large helping of steak and chips before a game.'

'Yes,' said Davey, 'But he was a prop forward and one of the hardest men ever to play the game. You're not.'

Bill smiled one of his smiles. 'Hello, Davey,' he said. 'That's why I'm sticking to the *crudités*. Looking forward to it?'

'Have you seen their forwards?' said Davey.

'Yes, big, aren't they?' said Al. 'Not surprisingly, really. Apparently most of the team are Paris *gardiens*.'

'*Gardiens*?' asked Tom. 'Police, prison warders, that sort of thing.' said Al. 'With a strong proportion of members of the CRS.'

'Ah,' said Peter. 'I somehow thought Pierre meant they were gardeners. CRS?'

'Riot police. They're the ones that don't take prisoners,' said Al, adding, I thought a little unnecessarily, 'That's the problem with you Brits. Monoglots.'

'What does he mean?' asked Tom.

Now Davey had mentioned it, though, I couldn't help noticing that the opposition were indeed rather big. My mind went back, as it often does at such times, to an away match when I was 13, against Nottingham High School. I don't know what it is about the East Midlands and early maturing, but these were giants. Our sports master took a look at them and said, 'Don't worry, lads, the bigger they come, the harder they fall'. But I could tell he wasn't entirely convincing himself or me. We lost heavily. But it didn't prevent me saying now, 'Don't worry, lads, the bigger they come, the harder they fall.'

' And they'll probably hear the wide one with the squint in Paris,' said Dan.'

'What's that tattoo on his neck say?' asked Jan.

'*Mort*,' said Al.

'I know what *mort* means,' said Tom. '*Bonne chance*.'

IT DIDN'T go that badly, to start with. The sun was shining. There were even spectators to whip up a bit of an atmosphere, including Pierce and Stew, as impassive in their shades as Tom in his brown ale and vin rouge. They were big, but we were defending surprisingly well. You could tell by the amount of grumbling that Davey was enjoying himself. Bill was dancing up and down on the wing, but, thankfully, neither ball nor opposition had reached him. Dan had managed what we like to call, I'm not sure why, several 'raking touch finders' (i.e. he had achieved a decent distance kicking the ball out of play in a forward direction). Jan had been giving him 'some decent service' (fast, accurate passes). Al, on the opposite wing to Bill, had gone on a couple of 'rampaging runs', supported by Peter, and, even, me. Unfortunately, Al, brought up on American Football, rarely passed the ball, except in a forward direction, so any move involving him did have a tendency to end with him. Harry was rushing around enthusiastically but to little effect, although the crowd were enjoying his frequent shouts of '*Allez!*'. The rest of us were doing our best, but something had to give.

It happened, predictably on Bill's wing. Monsieur Mort, he of the tattoo, had become an increasing presence. He was a man of impressive strength, both in physique and aroma, as I could vouch for, playing against him in the front row of the scrum. He also had face stubble of the consistency of sandpaper, which made the cheek-to-cheek experience which is such an integral part of propping particularly challenging, along with his muttered imprecations. (Why anyone should actually want to play prop is a discussion for another time; let me just say for the moment that sport does not have too many opportunities for the round, slow and short-legged who still dream).

M Mort now ran, or rather rumbled, up the right wing, and rounded Bill, who, in contrast to an adverb often used appreciatively of other threequarters, was deceptively slow. But no one could question his commitment to the cause, as he managed to recover and jump on M Mort's back. The only way, however, to stop players like M Mort is to tackle them round the legs: Bill was simply carried along without making any noticeable impact on the big man's progress. Now he faced the last man left, Davey. Davey went in for the tackle unhesitatingly, as was his custom; but the matter was complicated by Bill, who crashed off on contact and landed on top of Davey, leaving M Mort to proceed to the try line. This was highly amusing for the uncommitted observer and the French crowd, less so for us, although Tom didn't seem to have noticed. Bill was up and hopping around pretty quickly; Davey lay still on the turf.

Then a remarkable thing happened. Jan came rushing up and fell to her knees next to Davey, cradling his head. 'Davey! Davey! Are you ok?' Even in the midst of the drama I sensed that her concern was greater than for the average team mate. Which was puzzling, as this was the disdained northern hairdresser whom I had not previously had in the frame as the answer to a scrum-half's dreams. Davey opened his eyes, then opened them wider. 'Jan!' he said, with wonder in his voice. 'Where is that big French bastard?'

'Never mind him,' said Jan, her voice gruffer than usual, 'Are you all right?'

'He's scored,' said Bill. 'I almost had him.'

I could tell Davey was a bit shaken, as he didn't even blink at this outrageous claim. He struggled to his feet, supported by

Jan, and made to walk behind the posts to wait for the delayed French conversion.

'No, Davey, you're going off,' said Jan, again in a different tone, urgent, worried. 'You've had a bad knock, you can't go on.'

Davey looked at her with a smiling awe that might have been concussion, but I wasn't sure, especially when he obediently allowed her to put his arm round her shoulder and help him off. The French applauded, except, naturally, for M Mort, who growled to me as he made his way back to their half for the kick-off, '*Grandes filles, eh, n'est-ce pas?*' He probably spoke truer than he knew, as the French, for all their national flapping about *l'amour* and *la difference*, didn't seem to have noticed that Jan, at least, was a girl, big or otherwise (otherwise, actually).

They missed the conversion; it was followed immediately by the whistle for half-time. We huddled on the pitch as Peter gave the half-time talk. I don't know whether you are familiar with half-time talks, but, generally, they require a suspension of the critical faculties, as they are mostly instructions to do what you are doing better and stop doing what you are doing worse, ignoring the reality of ability, always accompanied by the speaker's fist being driven hard into his other palm, and ending with the exhortation that, however unlikely, 'We can win this one!'

This time, though, I felt that Peter had a point. A rugby team is an interesting entity: it has a dynamic that is almost mystical, transcendental, like an orchestra, although with chubbier fingers. Sometimes, the force is with you. A unity, a directed common purpose, flows strongly and builds a thrilling momentum throughout the 15, small, tall, round, slow, fit, fast or panting. But it is, by this nature, a fragile thing that can be easily upset; and this is easy in a game featuring a ball whose shape is designed to make it behave unpredictably, create confusion, prompt error and stifle this flow.

To counter that – and the other side, of course – there is what we call 'team spirit', the concentration on victory and refusal to contemplate defeat that has never been better summoned and conjured than by Shakespeare for Henry before Agincourt (the Bard would surely have been a fly-half). You can see these patterns clearly in most top class matches, including the said Agincourt, Waterloo, and, lest I seem a touch Francophobic, Jutland, the mighty sea battle between the British and German fleets where Admiral Beatty railed against the inexplicable absence of the force that any fan can feel when his or her team is struggling: 'There's something wrong with our bloody ships today'.

But this today I was feeling the opposite: great things were possible. First, though, we had to solve the problem of Davey's absence. Jan was sitting with him on the touchline. Even the French had noticed that she was holding his hand. I like to think they found this a little unsettling; they were certainly shrugging more than usual. Unfortunately, if predictably, all Peter's plans had failed to provide an adequate number of reserves, or even, frankly, one, especially as we'd lost the two Australians in Paris, and, it also transpired, when Peter wasn't looking, a Scotsman. Nor was it the kind of game which would permit borrowing a player from the opposition.

It was Harry who came up with the answer: 'The motorbike bloke looks like he could play a bit, doesn't he?' Peter stalked over to Stew and had a word. I could tell from the nods that it was going well. Stew was tall, but not big, thin. Before long, he was on the pitch and lining up at full back in borrowed kit in Davey's place. Odd short socks, too short shorts and Peter's reserve emergency shirt and trainers weren't the greatest look.

'He says he's played a bit,' said Peter, 'Quite keen, really'.

'At least he's not Pierce,' said Dan.

'Actually, Pierce is getting changed now,' said Peter. 'He hasn't really played but wouldn't mind a crack if we're desperate'.

In my experience, the Welsh accent has few rivals for expressing succinct disgust. 'Christ,' said Dan. 'And where's bloody Jan?'

Jan was back on the pitch, and, after a fond backward glance at Davey and a challenging forward glance at the rest of us, proceeded to play the game of her life. Even Dan was impressed, and she wasn't Welsh. That momentum I was talking about began to build. There was a rare take by Harry in the line out, leaping like a middle-aged salmon. The ball went to Jan, and from her to Dan; a sharp pass from him sent Al careering down the touchline at his most thunderous. No one was going to stop him, so the passing issue wasn't one, although we had to shout to remind him that he needed to touch the ball down, an oxymoronic irrelevance in the American version. Dan added the extras with aplomb (i.e. he converted the try, worth five points, into a goal, worth seven points, by kicking the ball through the posts.) We were ahead five minutes in and feeling good.

Very good. This was it: force and spirit concentrated in harmony. You begin to believe you're better than you are, and you start to play like it. I caught the ball from the French kick-off; instead of just standing my ground like a lump and waiting for a maul to form around me as usual, I fired out a pass to Dan. A pass so good, and so exceptional for me, that I can bring it back to mind any time I choose. Dan then executed the rarest of feats for him, the much-mentioned but barely sighted Neath Grammar School dummy, a feinted pass (in his version at least) that is so telegraphed and so obviously a dummy that it double-bluffs the defence.

Dan was through. He waited for a French defender to commit to tackling him before slipping it to Jan at his elbow. She stepped inside another defender then flung a splendid pass to Peter who had moved up on the right. A forward in space, exposed without the comfort of his team mates, often panics and kicks the ball. Indeed, this was what Peter usually did, but today he took the tackle, and slipped the ball out of the back of his hand to Al, who was coming up on a well-timed run.

Al charged through but was brought down by some determined tackling. The ruck formed, the ball appeared before Jan, and she had the option of a long pass to Bill, left unmarked on the other wing by defenders needed elsewhere. Bill juggled with it for, as we also say in the sports game, what seemed like an eternity before holding on and running over the try line, placing the ball firmly.

By the gods of the oval ball, it was exhilarating: united purpose, impromptu but determined, confidence oozing through us all like a universal elixir, unusual risks taken and coming off: if there's a finer example than rugby of the thrill, joy and nobility of concerted humanity not normally involving death or sex, I've never found it. Later, Bill confided that it was the first try he had ever scored. Dan repeated his extras with even more aplomb.

'Come on!' cried Peter. '*Allez!*' shouted Harry. But the French were far from finished. *Non.* Their forbidding forwards were beginning to rumble, guided expertly round the pitch by Pierre, who was playing opposite Jan at scrum half. I was doing my best, but my questionable stamina and M Mort's unquestionable strength were beginning to tell. Pierre made a darting break but was pulled down by Jan. As he fell, though, he managed to get a pass away to M Mort's partner in the front row, whom we shall call M Monstre.

This forbidding figure showed a good turn of speed; only Stew, our emergency fullback, stood in the way of a try. Displaying an unorthodox tackling technique, he seemed to slip as he rushed bravely in, and ended up sliding across the pitch legs first towards M Monstre, who simply hurdled them and strode on to the try line. 'Sorry, lads,' shouted Stew. 'Timing's a bit rusty'.

Pierre somehow contrived to miss the conversion again, but that's the French for you, gifted but (another key sporting description) mercurial. I think Pierce's sudden, arresting, quivering, high-volumed and entirely innocent coughing fit on the touchline as Pierre ran up to kick might have had something to do with it as well, if Pierre's look was anything to go by. We were still in the lead, 14-10, but the force was fleeing as swiftly and magically as it had arrived. The French had it, and were pressing. We faltered, like a tight rope walker looking down. The early start and the coach trip were catching up on us. Dan was caught in a tackle, fell awkwardly, and didn't get up. He'd turned his ankle and was helped off. I heard that one word – 'Christ' – again as Pierce shuffled on in his place, only to shuffle straight off again to give Tom his shades.

After hurried discussion, Pierce took his place on the opposite wing to Bill with his customary disturbing calm, and Al came in to fly half. I tried to point out that putting a player who couldn't pass at fly half is unconventional at best, but Peter would have none of it. 'Napoleon,' he said. 'The art of war is to confuse your opponent.' He was about to expound further when the referee, who had been surprisingly lenient, given he was both French and a referee, told us to get on with it.

There must have been 15 minutes to go. The French, I fancied, were beginning to get a bit cocky, which was not necessarily a good thing. Their fly half, irritatingly elegant in the Gallic way, danced round Al and veered off to the right. Peter, who was playing out of his skin, got back across and challenged him; he released the ball perfectly to his wing, a slight but tricky runner who dodged first this way and this. No one could get a finger on him and by now he had only Pierce to beat, who didn't seem to have noticed. Harry yelled 'Pierce!'; the winger feinted left and was just stepping right off his left foot when Pierce took a step forward, head-butted him, caught him as he was falling and tossed him over the touch line.

There was a paused moment of shock, and then most of the French were surrounding him in an angry melee, Pierce throwing punches in every direction. The referee was not lenient.

He gave Pierce what we like to call his marching orders. The *gardiens* retreated, muttering, but Pierce showed every sign of standing his ground and was still in attack position, on the balls of his feet, pushing out rapid shadow left-right combinations.

'You've got to go, Pierce,' I told him. 'You've been sent off.'

'Fair enough,' said Pierce. 'I haven't had so much fun since that stage invasion in Frisco. Peace and love, my arse. I could throw them further in those days, though.'

Harry was talking to Pierre and apologising to the *gardiens* for Pierce's '*non-sportif brusque de sang a la tete*'. They looked puzzled; Harry told me later he was referring to a 'rush of blood to the head'.

The referee awarded a penalty try, converted by Pierre: the French now led 17-14 with five minutes to go. Keen to further avenge the Pierce outrage, they upped their intensity. We kept them out for a couple of moves with luck and a long clearing kick from Jan. Then their fly half made another break, but was met by Peter with such force that the ball popped out of his hands and straight into Al's. The French recognised the danger and closed him down immediately. I grimaced as he shaped to pass, but, for once, he hadn't hurled it forwards, but sideways. He denied it afterwards but I'm pretty sure it was because he was slightly off balance. Anyway, it travelled a prodigious distance in the American Football fashion, towards where Stew, showing unexpected anticipation, had moved up quickly from full back.

Stew rose above two covering French defenders and appeared to hang in the air before sending a long looping header between the French goalposts. As he wheeled away, arm raised in triumph, Jan, following up quickly, fell on the ball over the line. Try!

Well, or I suppose I should say, *eh bien*, or, even, *sacre bleu*. We all went mad, and the French went mad, but for different reasons. We were ecstatic at what seemed an improbable victory; they were outraged at such a flagrant breach of the rules. I've studied it since – I've had a lot of time – and while not technically illegal, to head the ball in such a fashion can be declared to be against the spirit of the game and so disallowed. M Le Ref, in this instance, didn't hesitate. It was a try.

M Le Ref was surrounded by irate *gardiens*, but neither flinched nor conceded. I was told later – it was a busy session in the bar – that he had been booked for a minor traffic infringement on his way to the match. Other versions suggested that the bonnet of his tractor – he was a farmer – had been dented by the CRS during the last bid to bring the city to a halt by travelling slowly round the Arc de Triomphe. But I am able to dismiss the claim that he was a student during the riots of 1968: I said 'Danny the Red?' to him in the bar afterwards and he replied that another glass of wine would be '*tres gentil, merci*'. Not, of course, that I'm suggesting for a moment that any of this would have had any bearing on his decision.

Whatever, on the pitch, matters got very heated; so much so that Jan had to interpose herself between the referee and M Mort and M Monstre, uttering the interesting line, 'You wouldn't hit a woman, would you?' She was then firmly removed from the action by the now recovered Davey, who instructed her, 'Come on, darling. They're not worth it'. Bemusement followed consternation, on both sides. I certainly wouldn't have put money on Davey saying 'darling' 80 minutes earlier, even if he was a hairdresser. Harry attempted the conversion, and, unsurprisingly, missed, although, again unsurprisingly, he later claimed it was a peace gesture. (It turned out, of course, that neither Stew nor Pierce had ever played before, although Stew had distinguished himself in the lower football leagues as what they like to call an uncompromising defender.)

WELL, AGAIN. *Eh, bien, encore.* You would think that nothing would heal the breach opened up by the train of events on the pitch. Rugby players have always liked the idea of leaving disagreements there, but this was pushing it a bit, especially given Pierce's intervention. There were few handshakes afterwards, and we were a little muted in the shower. In the bar, studied politeness by us and deep glowering from them prevailed until Harry patched it up. He took Pierce and Stew over. His explanation of Pierce's behaviour was much helped by Pierce's demeanour – here was a man who had clearly lost the capacity even to spell malice. The Pierce-affected winger, Julian, thankfully seemed to bear no grudge, which wouldn't have been the case if Pierce had attacked me. *Entente* was becoming progressively more *cordiale* until we noticed M Mort approaching at pace from outside. He flung the doors open and approached us at a purpose, then pronounced the magic words: '*Trop Tard Le Tourniquet!?*' He then took off his teeshirt to reveal another, this time familiar, tattoo of the headless corpse and the blood. I shall never again need confirmation of culture's ability to cross boundaries and unite former foes.

Harry, naturally, was now in his element, and Stew's mime of his winning header, together with shrugs and basic French – 'Me, *moi*, not rugby player, footballer, Bobby Charlton, David Beckham, very nice, *tres gentil*, but *pas tres intelligent*, *pas* the sharpest *oignons* in the *casserole*' – went down very well.

Al was circulating in best civilised American fashion, emphasising the US debt to Lafayette and the French in 1776, and confiding that he, as a banker, understood very well the need for a riot squad. Bill, who had never displayed any ability to pace himself, except on the wing, slowly, had embarked on some serious communing with M Armagnac which, fortunately, rendered completely incomprehensible his attempts to impress on M Mort how he would get him *les temps prochaine*. I managed to persuade Tom that he should keep to himself for now the theory that the French took defeat better than we did because they were more used to it. Jan and Davey were in a corner, still holding hands. We had by now abandoned all attempts to explain that they weren't gay, as it seemed simpler, and not that important. None of us had seen it coming, except Dan, who was resting his ankle with Pernod. 'The bond between fly-half and scrum-half is almost psychic,' he said. 'I knew something was on her mind because her box kicking was suffering. It's the little things.'

By now Peter was fussing about getting us to sit down to dinner, as we were fast approaching the point at which we entered this story: indeed, Harry and the trousers. It is a tribute to the unique camaraderie of the rugby team that Jan managed to tear herself away from Davey to take part in The Muffin Man; he was under strict orders to take it easy. I wasn't sure what was the most startling, his happy and unprecedented acceptance of advice, or his continuing constant smile, previously unsighted except for the briefest of muscle movements, usually provoked by the latest southern idiocy.

Other highlights of a long night would be the broom cupboard off the main room slowly swinging open on its hinges to reveal a prostrate Bill and then slowly swinging back shut again, repeated every five minutes or so; Peter, remarkably relaxed, saying to me on his way out, 'Goodnight, Charles. Good old Harry. I'm going to look up at the stars'; and Tom's striking ability to remain amiably unmoved by drink, emotion, affection or anything, really. The singing was good, too, although M Mort, Harry and Pierce singing *Entrail Blues* yet again did pall. I shall not easily forget the CRS members with tears running down their faces as they belted out the company's song, '*Sur La Tete, Mon Fils*'. But nothing moved me quite like Al singing '*I Wish I Knew How It Would Feel To Be Free*'. I sensed that he would not long be a banker, even though he claimed it was about tariff barriers.

I was among the last carousers, and swayed off on the short walk to the home of none other than M Mort. This, as I should surely have expected, was done out in the best minimalist taste, with bookshelves boasting Sartre and De Beauvoir. As he bade me goodnight after showing me to my room, M Mort took me by the shoulders, looked into my eyes and intoned with great solemnity, '*Ce que, finalement, je sais de plus sûr sur la morale et les obligations des hommes, c'est au football que je le dois.*' 'Ah, yes,' I said, 'Camus: "All I know most surely about morality and obligations, I owe to football."' I didn't mention my easy familiarity arose from a popular teeshirt among the more cerebral British football fans. But I did venture the thought that if Camus had played rugby, he might not have developed the despair that led to his ideas on Absurdism, as there is an essential truth, meaning and beauty to the oval game that is not to be discovered elsewhere, certainly not in the false constraints and frustrations of the alternative code, which vetoes our most basic aid to understanding, the hand that turns the page or clicks the mouse. 'In short, *mon ami*,' I concluded, 'if Albert had picked it up and run with it, he would have found happiness'.

I was a little drunk, and had forgotten that Camus was, in fact, a goalkeeper, which rather ruined the thesis. M Mort smiled and intoned even more solemnly, '*On reconnaît son cours en découvrant les chemins qui éloignent d'elle*'. I nodded equally solemnly and thought it was an odd time to be talking about trains, especially when we were travelling by coach. Any further discussion, however, was terminated by the appearance of Madame Mort, who, it did not surprise me to learn, was also in the CRS; neither of us saw fit to quibble with her firm indication that it was bedtime. Next day, on the coach back home, Harry was able to enlighten me on M Mort's apercu. 'Oh, yes, good old Cammers,' he said. 'One recognises one's course by discovering the paths that stray from it'. This seemed to cover the guiding philosophy of both rugby and riot policemen. I thought of M Mort with a new respect, particularly for his sensitive forbearance from mentioning the goalkeeping.

THE JOURNEY BACK went quite well, to begin with. Pierce was driving imperturbably as usual. Stew and Bill had secured their bike to the back on the bull-horn fenders The Tourniquet had thoughtfully provided and were taking it easy inside. Davey and Jan were sitting quietly and talking intensely. 'Now your feather cut can be a bit tricky,' I heard him tell her as I passed on my way to talk to Harry. Dan had thought up a rather good wheeze: we were having a sweepstake on what time Harry would fall asleep, as he always did on coach journeys, especially ones with a night like the last. Harry, naturally, was not informed of the competition, but we were allowed to influence the result by talking to him, which I was doing fairly regularly, having drawn three hours and two minutes. Actually, I should say by listening to him; in any case, I had learnt quite a lot about such varied topics as promissory estoppel, the superiority of German supermarket groups, the flora and fauna of Guatemala, WHV 'Hopper' Levett, the Kent and England wicketkeeper, and when to wear brown shoes. On reflection, though – did I mention I've had a lot of time for that? – it was unwise to include Pierce in the draw. Harry sailed past my mark and was only starting to flag around four hours, as we closed in on Calais. Pierce had four hours and 37 minutes and was getting increasingly agitated as that moment neared. So it was that after shouting 'Harry!' twice and getting no reply at four hours and 33, he turned round to see what was going on with our favourite solicitor.

The crash was inevitable. The coach was a terrible mess. I can still recall with sad ease Tom the owner weeping when he arrived to survey the wreckage of his dream acquisition, tangled and mangled by the side of the Route Nationale; all that was left visible and intact of the splendid coachwork was a still defiant Tag giving his two finger salute. We all survived, after a fashion. Harry still talks a lot; Jan and Davey still stare into one another's eyes; Dan drinks Pernod steadily but with diminishing enthusiasm; and I'm working my way through what seem like endless beers as I try yet again to explain technical offences in the ruck to Tom. Al still dreams of the perfect leveraged outcome, which refuses to come. Peter hops from one foot to the other, endlessly waiting for the other side. I'm prevented by convention from telling you too much more, but, as you probably know, there's a certain amount of atonement, proportionate to past conduct, required before one can move on up to the big HQ, what we might call Twickenheaven. What I hadn't realised is that, for administrative purposes, and in these sort of circumstances, it's a team thing. Which means, basically, we're still waiting on Bill, not to mention Stew; and, of course, Pierce. Several of our bit players have also turned out to be a bit dodgy. As you will have gathered, I've always been a good team player, but it's impossible not to wonder whether, in the end, despite the laughs, it was worth it, especially with what we're doing now. Haunting, really.

Tom Pierce, Tom Pierce, lend me your grey mare.
All along, down along, out along lea.
For I want for to go to Widecombe Fair,
With Bill Brewer, Jan Stewer, Peter Gurney,
Peter Davey, Dan'l Whiddon, Harry Hawke,
Old Uncle Tom Cobley and all,
Old Uncle Tom Cobley and all.
And when shall I see again my grey mare?
All along, down along, out along lea.
By Friday soon, or Saturday noon,

With Bill Brewer, etc
So they harnessed and bridled the old grey mare.
All along, down along, out along lea.
And off they drove to Widecombe fair,
With Bill Brewer, etc
Then Friday came, and Saturday noon.
All along, down along, out along lea.
But Tom Pierce's old mare hath not trotted home,
With Bill Brewer, etc
So Tom Pierce he got up to the top o' the hill.
All along, down along, out along lea.
And he seed his old mare down a-making her will,
With Bill Brewer, etc
So Tom Pierce's old mare, her took sick and died.
All along, down along, out along lea.
And Tom he sat down on a stone, and he cried
With Bill Brewer, etc
But this isn't the end o' this shocking affair.
All along, down along, out along lea.
Nor, though they be dead, of the horrid career
Of Bill Brewer, etc
When the wind whistles cold on the moor of the night.
All along, down along, out along lea.
Tom Pierce's old mare doth appear ghastly white,
With Bill Brewer, Jan Stewer, Peter Gurney,
Peter Davy, Dan'l Whiddon, Harry Hawke,
Old Uncle Tom Cobley and all,
Old Uncle Tom Cobley and all.

+++
SOMETHING BLUE
+++

JACKET REQUIRED +++

PETER TIPPED the brow of his hat forward, so that it shaded his eyes. He rocked back in his chair and prepared to zed the afternoon away. It would make a change from staring out of the window. But it would still be hot, had been for weeks. The kind of heat that was made for long afternoons in dirty motels, the kind of dirty motels where the ice machine was always broken and the owner always had a secret. Peter had been in a lot of motels like that. But now he was going to sleep. If his mind would let him. If his memories would let him.

Sodor. Almost exactly the right name for it. If you liked trains, it had something going for it. Peter didn't like trains. Something about the straight lines, and the catering. So why Sodor? It was a question he asked himself all the time, like now. A question with an answer lost behind a haze of cheap scent and strong drink hiding a history of soft voices and wrong calls. And now he was here, on an island where they called the trains names like Thomas. Where they called everything names, including Lennie the Lamp Post and Reggie the Roundabout, come to that. It had come to that. And Peter still wasn't asleep. He reached for the bourbon bottle.

Suddenly, a bell rang furiously in the outer office. Voices were raised, but not in happy hallelujah. Flopsy Bunny rushed in. For once, her ears were erect, and quivering. 'Canyabelieveit?'she shouted. 'Liddle guy comes in and gooses me! Gooses me! Just like that. Says he's got a problem but first he's going to help me out!'

'So did he?' asked Peter, laconically. Laconically went with the territory, like the dust and the regrets.

'Did he?!' said Flopsy. 'Guy's got another problem now, like whether to clutch his testicular accessories, nurse his big toe or hold his jaw in place.'

'And the bell?' asked Peter. 'What's with the bell? We haven't got a bell.'

'No, but he has. On his hat.' Peter sighed. It was the kind of sigh you had to earn. 'Send him in,' he said.

Flopsy went out and ushered the visitor in with a glare straight off Route 66 at noon. The visitor had gone for the accessories and jaw option. He was limping. On his head was a hat with a bell on the end. He looked at Peter. 'Christ,' he said. 'That's all I need. Another rabbit.'

Peter smiled the smile of a rabbit for whom rabbitism was nothing new. It was a thin smile, this smile; and his ears were very still. 'Listen, small fry,' he said. 'Before I made with the aspersions I'd wonder about the wisdom of wearing lederhosen with knees like yours. Also, I could ask Flopsy Bunny to come in.'

'Okay, okay,' said the little man. 'Keep your tail on. I've got nothing against rabbits personally. Some of my best friends have had big ears. Hey, she's all woman, that Flopsy. And what a left! No, look, it's just, well, PR-PI, I didn't think, I mean, forgive me, I ain't ever seen a fedora with ears before, and, well, how can I put this, rabbits are not exactly legendary for being the business in a tight spot. If I was to mention headlights, you know?'

Peter smiled the smile again. 'What's your name?' he asked. 'Noddy,' said the little man. 'Well, Noddy,' said Peter, 'This is Sodor, my friend. If you want a gumshoe, there's me, or there's the Teletubbies. So, you want some simpering unintelligible indeterminates who have trouble finding the business end of a vacuum cleaner, or you want a rabbit who's been around the warren a bit?' Noddy took off his hat. The bell rang loudly in the heat and the silence. Noddy was bald, and he was sweating.

'Okay, Peter,' he said, 'Okay.' His eyes hit the bourbon like a camel at an oasis. 'Any chance of a drink?' Peter reached down into the desk drawer for another tumbler, gave it a polish on his blue jacket, poured them both large ones, and waited. 'Do you know Toytown, Peter?' asked Noddy. His tumbler was empty, emptied with all the furtive ease and nudging guilt of the heavy drinker. His hands had stopped shaking now but he was still sweating.

'I knew someone there,' said Peter, 'Once.' An almost imperceptible twitch of the left ear above the fedora was the only indication of what that someone might have meant to him.

'So you'll know that it is not all sunny smiles and dumb animals. And, boy are they dumb. You'll know there's hurt and hate, too, and fear and loneliness that tears hearts. Oh, yes, believe me, Peter, Toytown has its dark side.' Noddy looked at the bottle again. Peter said nothing. Another sad little guy with problems. On the whole, he thought, he'd rather be staring out of the window. But that didn't pay the rent, or pay for the drink that helped him forget. Helped him forget people like that someone in Toytown. On the good days. Noddy was still talking in his high-pitched voice. Maybe that was the result of his brush with Flopsy. Maybe it wasn't.

'So, I drive a cab in Toytown. It's a living, and you get to meet people. I do pretty well with the ladies. You might laugh, but a cap with a bell on the end is one hell of an icebreaker. You might be right about the shorts, though, could be I am getting a little old for this look. How about some skinny jeans, what do you think?'

'I think it depends how much time you've got,' said Peter. 'And dough. I've got all day, but I charge ten gems an hour and that's a lot of lettuce.'

Noddy nodded, nervous. Peter was glad he'd taken his hat off. 'You're right, I should get to the point. They're trying to kill me. It's because I know too much. And now they know I know and they're trying to kill me.'

The telephone rang in the outer office. Noddy hit the floor, fast. There was a muffled answering ring as he landed on his hat. This guy was nervous, all right. Flopsy came in. 'A Mrs Bump was on. I told her we don't do divorce. What are you doing down there? I didn't hit you that hard.'

This last was to Noddy, who was still on the floor. He got to his feet, holding up his hands. 'Steady, sister,' he said, 'I'm not packing nothing.' 'I can see that,' said Flopsy on her way out. 'I told you about the shorts,' said Peter.

Noddy got back in his seat. Peter levelled a stare that wasn't completely unsympathetic. Sometimes in this business, you had to humour people, even ones in shorts with a bell.

'It's the bears,' said Noddy.

'The bears,' repeated Peter, slowly. 'What bears, Noddy?'

Noddy flashed a look of the old wise-guy truculence. 'Wise up, bunny,' he said. 'You must have noticed. You're supposed to be a shamus, for chrissake. Bears are everywhere. These are the guys who dominate kiddies' fiction. Big bears, small bears, fat bears, cuddly bears, funny bears. Nothing moves without the bears. Let me give you Rupert Bear, Baloo the Bear, Sooty and The Three Bears for six. You can think of the rest, the Care guys, the Gummis, the two dumb ones in Yellowstone Park, the Latin American with the all-day breakfast habit. Wise up, Bunny, and smell the radishes. The bears are the mob. Just squint around! You name it, the bears run it: Toytown, Trumpton, Balamory, Wimbledon Common, Greendale, Nutwood, the Thirteen Acre Wood, every frigging wood, all of it! And if you get in their way, it's the big pie in the sky for you and the big toy box for me. You better believe it, fluffy tail.'

Peter was all ears now. Maybe he was out of touch, here on Sodor. He'd come to the island to forget; perhaps he'd been too thorough. 'Wimbledon Common?' he said. 'The Wombles run Wimbledon Common, everyone knows that.'

Noddy shook his head, overplaying the mournful stare. This was not a subtle guy. 'Peter! Baby! Don't tell me you've fallen for that one. They may call themselves Wombles, but look closely, they're bears!'

A trickle of sweat ran down Peter's spine and met a shiver coming the other way. 'And what's with this Thirteen Acre Wood?'

Noddy chuckled, but it wasn't a happy Toytown kind of chuckle. 'That's all that's left of the Hundred Acre Wood after The Pooh sold off the rest for housing. He's some bruin that one. Don't you fall for that little brain schmooze. Nothing moves in the Thirteen Acre without Winnie's say-so. You think honey grows on trees? You think those sticks ain't fixed? Please!'

Peter stood up and walked to the window for a long stare. Behind him he knew Noddy had put his hat back on from the ringing. Maybe this nervous punk was right to be a nervous punk. Peter hadn't trusted his guts, once. He was young and the gardener was old and angry if incomprehensible. He'd got away with it that time, but he had lost his first blue jacket. Now he always trusted his guts and kept some spare jackets. So that was why it was so quiet on Sodor. The action was all elsewhere. And maybe he liked it like that. The bell brought him back to reality, and his bank account. Peter filled the little man's glass, again. 'Deal me some more, Noddy.'

'It was about a week ago. In Toytown, obviously. I had that Mrs Tubby Bear in the cab. With Big Winnie. Very tight fit. And a lot of weight. Never got out of first. Winnie was on a visit. He didn't say much, just kept chewing on his stogie. That's something else they don't tell you about Winnie, his Havana habit. Anyway, I took them to Pinocchio's for lunch – you won't believe the prices in that joint – and waited outside. The window was open and Big Ears has got, well, big ears. No offence by the way, Peter. So Big Ears heard everything. The Bears are up for expansion. And the place they've got eyes on is here, the good old island of Sodor. That railway is a goldmine, says Mrs TB. It's just ticking over at the moment, she says, run by this fat guy who's so smart and clued up he spends most of his time talking to the engines. Mrs TB tells Winnie they could go big, hike the fares, launder the narcotics money through it, who knows, put in some gaming machines, turn those antique old stations into casinos. All we gottado, she says, is rub out the fat guy. Trust me, she says, the engines will complain, and jeez do those engines complain, but they'll do what they're told. Not much going on in those smoke boxes, let me assure you. Why don't we have our picnic over there, she says, and combine some business with pleasure? And Winnie, he just wheezed in that unpleasant way and said it all sounded like pleasure to him.'

Peter needed the next sip. 'I see. But why don't you go to the pigs? Fill them in with your suspicions?'

'The Pigs!?' cried Noddy. 'They're the other outfit: Pinky and Perky, Babe, Piglet, Pigling Bland, Wilbur, Preston, the three little ones – and that's before you get to Peppa and her family!'

'Ok,' said Peter. 'Ok. Easy, little fella. I didn't mean the kind of pig that ends up on a plate complementing cabbage. Let me adjust my vernacular. Why didn't you go to Plod?'

'We did! And now my big-hearted and even bigger-eared friend is dead! Bushwhacked on the main street, just outside Mr Jumbo's house! Those seriously major ears will hear no more. Plod's on the Bears' payroll and I'm on the run. You gotta help me, Ears!' He was mixing sobs with nods now. There was quite a noise. 'And there's no time – Friday's the day the teddy bears have their picnic!'

Peter's right ear twitched, like it always did when the heat was on and the fan was off. 'That's tomorrow. What's their plan for rubbing out the Fat C?'

'Hey, what do you do for your lettuce?' said Noddy with a flash of the old bravado. 'That's for you to find out, Whiskers. I've done my bit. I've risked my life and lost my friend. I'm going to lie low while you get these guys off my poor little back. If you want me, there's a club just outside Nutwood city limits, The Blue Peter. Lot of characters hang out there. There's a waitress, Rosie, she'll get a message to me. Might be a place to pick up more griff on the bears, too.'

'The Blue Peter?' said Peter. 'Sounds pretty raunchy.'

'Trust me,' said Noddy.

Neither of them had noticed the office door opening just wide enough to give a Magnum room to call. Noddy's bell rang for the last time. The little guy was lying low, all right, permanently. Ice cream was everywhere. Peter hopped it fast to the outer office. There was no one in it. No one alive, that is. Flopsy's cry had been drowned by that damn bell. Peter intoned the relevant lines from Donne. He was funny like that. But he wasn't smiling. He pushed the door back into his office. There was something sticky on the doorknob which he couldn't immediately identify. No point calling the Police: they'd been letting Thomas and his friends get away with murder for years. Peter narrowed his eyes and contemplated his situation. He had no client now. Sure, he owed plenty, but he owed Flopsy more. Poor lovely totally incompetent Flopsy. He reached into his drawer, took out a carrot and put it into the shoulder holster beneath his famous blue jacket. He was going to make some calls of his own.

THE DRIVE TO Nutwood was relieved by the sweet but sad way with a trumpet employed by one of Peter's favourites, Bunny Berigan, on the car player. 'I can't get started with you,' crooned Bunny, and Peter nodded, remembering. He located the Blue Peter without difficulty and parked his Courgette beyond where the neon sign was flashing on and off, like his luck. There was a bear on the door. Peter pointed a paw at the sign reading, 'No Elves. No Pirates. And Especially No Superheroes.' 'Can't handle their drink. Terrible outfits,' growled the bear. He took Peter's money just like the bored Siamese on reception took his money. Inside was like more clubs than Peter cared to recall. Low lights concealed identities, secrets and a considerable amount of fluff on the carpets. A combo bearing a startling resemblance to Andy Pandy (keyboards), Bill the Flowerpot Man (double bass), Noggin the Nog (sax) and Crystal Tipps (vocals) were playing to a clientele more interested in the bottom of their glasses than *'You're a Pink Toothbrush, I'm a Blue Toothbrush'*. It wasn't difficult to spot Rosie, even though there was no sign of Jim. The years hadn't been kind and the eyes were deader than ever.

'What can I do for you, Ears?'

'Vodka and Carrot, one cube. How's Jim?'

'Don't talk to me about that schmuck. He's living with a lock keeper near Devizes. Do I know you? You look like all the other rabbits to me.'

'No, you don't know me. Noddy sent me. Thought you might be able to help me with some lowdown on our bear friends and certain adjustments and dispositions they might be making.'

'Noddy! How is the little guy? Not so little everywhere, believe me.' Rosie smirked, which was not attractive. 'How's his nerves? Still troubling him?'

'No. He's found a permanent cure for his nerves.'

'That's swell. You want to know about our bear friends, talk to one of them. Sooty's over there. He knows a lot more than he lets on. Say, you're pretty cute yourself, for a hopper. I'll get your drink.'

'What's Sooty drinking?'

'Guinness. By the bucket. You know what glove puppets are like. Hollow insides. I thought Postman Pat could knock it back, but Sooty leaves them all behind.'

'A Guinness for my new best friend as well, please.'

'As you like, bunny boy.'

Peter waited, looking. The Blue Peter was a good place to look. If you wanted to check on casualties from the battle to put a sparkle in a kid's eye and some weight in other people's wallets. Over in another corner, well into a bottle, was Tintin, face flushed, running to fat now, podgy hand running up the thigh of a bored looking Lady Penelope. Crystal and gang finished their set, to that patchy smatter of half-hearted applause more depressing than silence.

Rosie returned with the drinks. 'Come back and see me when you've finished with the Sootster,' she said.

'Honey,' said Peter, trying to make contact with the dead eyes. 'You're a rag doll. I'm a rabbit. Doesn't take too much internal above-chin activity to work out that this is not a working hypothesis.'

'I love it when you make with the the big-word action, Ears.' Rosie placed a lot of emphasis on 'big', which didn't do it for Peter, either. Something about class.

Peter put the Guinness down next to Sooty. Sooty didn't look up from the one he was staring into. 'Sooty? I'm Peter Rabbit. You might have heard of me.' Sooty still didn't look up, but he spoke, in a very low whisper which was also surprisingly harsh. 'Sure I've heard of you. You're the private dick, right, the one whose old man ended up in the pastry overcoat? Well, you won't get Sooty to talk. Whisper a little, but that's all.'

'Why haven't you ever talked, Sooty?' said Peter. 'A big star like you should have respect. People would want to hear what you've got to say. The broad with you on the show, she talks a lot. And the little dog that squeaks. But we want to hear you.'

'With this voice?' rasped Sooty. 'You're kidding me. You're right about respect though. That's what I don't get. Not from Soo, not from Sweep, and especially not from Little Cousin Scampi.'

It was karaoke time up on stage now. Babar was murdering *'My Way'*. 'Respect,' whispered Sooty again. 'That's what I don't get. I told Winnie if he wanted to rub out the fat train guy, it should be clean and it should be quick and there should be no bears appearing anywhere in the vicinity. So he said, nuts, Sooty, you're a little guy and you'll always be a little guy because you think like a little guy. Who's going to touch us? We're the bears!'

Babar had now moved on to *'New York, New York'* together with his chum Dumbo, who was really flying. Sooty was singing, too, but in another way.

'So Winnie didn't appreciate your advice?'

Sooty snorted into his Guinness. Some froth stuck to his snout, but he didn't seem to notice.'Oh, that Winnie's much too much of a big shot to listen to me. What have I ever done? How many times has he played Blackpool to a half-full house of snotty kids high on extra strength candy floss? Middle class creep. He wants it all. That's a bear as won't be happy until there's a bear in every line of every story. And if that means a few innocent rabbits, kittens, squirrels, owls, toads and water rats have to die, he don't care that much.'

Peter whistled, which was a mistake, as they were immediately joined by Mutley, Lassie and Rover. Big drinkers and terrible bores. Once you've heard about one incredible rescue achieved against all odds by supreme canine intelligence, thought Peter, you tended to have heard them all. Thank goodness Snowy had retired to Wagga Wagga. Peter asked them what they were drinking. 'Hair of the dog,' shouted Rover; Mutley went into the wheeze. Peter wondered just how many times Mutley had heard that one. A lot more times than Peter had enjoyed his lousy cartoon. He waved at Rosie. Lassie was already telling the one with the canyon, the broken bridge, the old clothes line and the unicycle. Sooty, sensibly, was ignoring them in favour of a resumed session of staring into his glass. 'Did I ever tell you how I saved Christmas?' asked Rover.

Sooty seemed to come to some sort of a decision. 'Let me,' he whispered to Peter, 'try to put some flickering illumination between those enormous sonic appendages of yours. Tell me, why would this year's teddy bears' picnic have been thrown open to all comers? Because the bears love you guys and would like for nothing better than to share our honey? Because Winnie can't bear to be separated from his chums, the insufferably wet English kid, the arrested pig, the single parent kangaroo family, the neurasthenic donkey, the tiger with Tourette's, and, pardon me, Ears, the OCD rabbit? Pete, I don't draw pictures, I just wave a wand around and mug a bit, but I think you by now might be nearing the conclusion to which I am driving, which is that everyone but the bears will be wasting money on a return ticket, seeing as the sort of jelly on offer may well be the sort that goes bang.'

Peter almost whistled again, but remembered just in time. This left his lips pursed and gave entirely the wrong signal to Rosie, who had arrived with three glasses of Beaune on her way with a very large one on the rocks for Barney the Dinosaur, who needed it after another challenging session of being loveable. Babar and Dumbo were well into the Dawn Patrol elephant song from '*Jungle Book*', accompanying 'Keep it up, up, up,' with appropriately obscene gestures. Peter suddenly felt very tired. He was also wondering why Sooty was telling him all this.

'You must be wondering why I'm telling you all this,' said Sooty. 'Pete, I'll tell you why I'm telling you all this. I'm telling you all this because I am tired of living a lie! I can talk and I will talk! And I am going to talk to the world about the bears!'

Sooty got up and began to make his way to the stage unsteadily, which was not all that surprising given he was legless. What happened next happened very quickly. Dumbo was showing off the trick where he fired peanuts simultaneously from his trunk and the other end. A stray fusillade caught Rosie just under the heart. She fell over backwards. Her tray went flying and with it Barney's comfort on the rocks. Sooty measured his length over a stray ice cube as Barney, desperate to save his hooch, fell on top of him. Even a young fit glove puppet would have had little chance of surviving the full weight of a large purple dinosaur, and Sooty had been in far too many conversations with Dr Booze for that. He never stood a chance. Squashed completely flat.

After a lot of effort and a little grandstanding, the two elephants managed to get Barney to his feet. Lady P came over, a little unsteadily. 'Poor little fellow,' she said. 'Maybe they could use him as a hot water bottle holder.' What a very cruel business this could be, thought Peter.

Barney, meanwhile, was telling anyone who'd listen that it had been a complete accident, that he was stone cold sober, he'd just slipped. He could see that killing Sooty was not necessarily a good career move. Maybe he could set up a Sooty Foundation for causes the little bear had championed, like compulsory manicures for puppeteers. Barney was sobbing now. Peter went over to the spot where he'd slipped. There was something sticky on the floor. Again. This guy was good. And tomorrow was the picnic.

PETER DROVE BACK to Sodor over the Jubilee Bridge and spent a few restless hours on his sofa. There'd been no time to hop into bed. He was up early; after a shower, two black coffees and five celery sticks he put on a clean blue jacket and made his way to Vicarstown station, where Bertie Bus was due to drop the picnickers for their outing on Thomas the Tank Engine. Thomas was waiting, building up a head of steam, with the usual vapid expression on his face. 'Thomas,' said

Peter. 'Hello, Peter!' said Thomas. 'Today is a very exciting day! It's the day the teddy bears have their picnic. And the Fat Controller has chosen me to take them! He could have chosen any of the engines, but he chose me. They're really jealous!'

'That's nice, Thomas,' said Peter. 'Anybody here yet?'

'Oh, yes! The bears are all waiting in the waiting room. The other guests are due soon. It's going to be a splendid picnic! There will be plenty of fun and food! And music! All the bears are carrying shiny instrument cases! I'm just waiting for Sir Topham to start us off!'

Jeez, thought Peter, not for the first time where Thomas was concerned. He took up a vantage point hidden behind a luggage cart on the opposite platform and waited, too. It wasn't long before Bertie Bus showed up. Peter watched. Most of the gang were there, with the exception, of course, of Noddy, Flopsy, and Sooty, who would never ride the iron horse again. There was the familiar commotion as the Tracys, in familiar fashion, jerkily arrived in their interminable Thunderbirds at the end of the platform. Jerks is so right, thought Peter.

Then he saw her. Lola. That beautiful crazy rabbit. So beautiful she could make this rabbit's heart turn over with one look. So crazy she had chosen Bugs Bunny over this rabbit. And broken this turned-over heart, permanently.

For a moment, Peter lost focus as Bunny Berigan played in his head and Beatrice Butterfly played in his belly. Then the bears appeared, all wearing dark glasses and demanding his attention. But not before he had noticed Lola was on her own, sans that pesky rabbit who was obviously on the lam yet again. What under the earth did she see in Bugs? Not his famous sense of humour, surely: he was about as funny as *Coniglio alla cacciatora.* But now the Fat Controller had arrived with the usual pomp and circumference. He was greeted by Winnie, who was exercising the faltering and fopping that no longer worked with this rabbit.

The bears and their guests climbed aboard. Quite a few had to be told twice, as concentration is not necessarily uppermost with these characters. Peter worked his way across to Thomas's hidden side in time to hear Winnie telling the Fat Controller to climb on board, beautiful day for it, top hole, the usual guff. Sir Topham was blithering on about logistical demands, timetable to finesse, engines to educate. And to provoke bickering among them with arbitrary and high-handed decisions which set children such a bad example, Peter added to himself, just a touch sanctimoniously. But that's often the way with noble knight-errant righters of wrongs. Winnie lost patience. 'Okay, Fatso. I'm through pussy-footing. Let's have some back-up here!' The steam that Thomas had rather ostentatiously been releasing all over the platform cleared to reveal a very big bear indeed, who was wearing what had to be hoped was a faux-fur coat. He was clearly carrying. Suddenly Peter understood: the sticky substance in his office and at The Blue Peter: porridge! Daddy Bear motioned to the FC; he embarked, fast. The big bear then leapt on to Thomas, ejecting the driver, who, nothing new, hadn't been playing much of a part. Daddy pulled some levers and Thomas began to move. His eyes were watering.

As the allegedly useful engine pulled out, Peter hopped on the back and made his way through the rear carriage. There were mostly nonbears in the seats, many of them juiced up already, oblivious to the plans that had been made for them. Christopher Robin was slumped, unshaven, mouth open, leaning against The Mad Hatter, who had his arm round Pansy Potter, the Strongman's Daughter. The Woodentops looked completely out of it, though with them it was always difficult to tell. Tigger was medicating. Rabbit and Ratty smiled up at Peter as he passed, but he put his carrot to his lips. He was looking for back-up, without much success. Where was Captain Hurricane or Desperate Dan when you really needed them? Come to that, where was Lassie? As he'd suspected, all bark.

'Ah, my buck-toothed friend. Tell me, do you have a ticket?' Rupert had come in from the front carriage and was blocking Peter's way. 'Sure thing, posh boy,' snarled Peter. 'It's one way, to Snoozeville.'

The young bear in the terrible trousers was hit by a hot cross from a bunny and went down at pace. Nutwood was safe from bad scans for a few hours at least. Peter stepped over him, ignoring the applause from the other seats. Nobody liked the bears. Employing sheer guts and all four legs, Peter manoeuvred himself out and up onto the roof, hopped to the front carriage and climbed down on Thomas. He moved along the engine's outside running plate, losing his fedora but not his poise. Another spring took him into Thomas and right behind Daddy Bear, who was leaning out the other side admiring the view. 'I've got a carrot and I'm not afraid to use it,' said Peter, lettuce cool.'Who's sticking something in my back?' shouted Daddy. 'Just a tired rabbit who needs a new secretary. Thomas, stop!' The steaming little machine, ever ready to grind to a halt, did. They got down and went back to the bears' carriage.

'He's got a carrot and he's not afraid to use it!' shouted Daddy Bear as they entered.

If Winnie was surprised, he didn't show it. 'Why don't you put the carrot down,' he said. 'You can't escape. There's too many of us. And we've gone too far to let you stop us. Tell him it's true, Lola.' She was sitting next to Winnie, smiling bravely. 'Tell him it's true, Lola, or will we have to persuade you, too?'

'Don't touch a hair of that rabbit!' shouted Peter.

'Poor old noble, romantic Peter,' said Winnie. 'In what world can you compete with us? Who are you working for? Yourself? That's the way to get rich, isn't it, big feet? Tell him, Lola.'

Lola blinked away some tears from her giant bewitching eyes. Peter played for time: 'So who are *you* working for, honey-sucker? And how wise is it to rub out so many favourites of so many of our young friends? The children will never forgive you. You'll be finished. Kaput. Iced. Exed. In five years, the only bears in fiction will be the bad ones, in bit parts. And how many movies do you suppose Leonardo DiCaprio can make? Don't even think about going for those oats in your pocket, Daddy. Sit down over there.'

'He's right, Winnie,' said the Fat Controller, who up until now had been sitting in a corner shaking slightly and failing by some measure to provide a good example to young readers of fortitude in the face of adversity. 'But it's not too late. I'll give you a couple of off-peak services on branch lines if you don't shoot me.'

Winnie laughed. It wasn't a pleasant sound. 'Please, my friends, wise up. Who do you imagine is paying us? I'll tell you: the parents are paying us! Yes! They're the ones who are demanding a bit more reality, more action, a bit more nastiness to prepare their kids for what's really out there! Haven't these miserable excuses for entertainment seen any shoot-em-up? We've got CGI now, you know. Parents are *so* fed up with your crap, your sickly sweet sledgehammer slices of illiterate burblings and corny morality. Don't forget, they're the ones who have to read them! Do you seriously think they like your incomprehensible Beatrix Potter stories with their non-existent plots and half-formed minor characters? Have you ever tried Squirrel Nutkin? Have you?'

Secretly, Peter had to agree. It was the reason he'd left. For a moment, he hesitated. The carrot wavered. It was all Daddy needed. His hand flashed to his pocket. But Lola was even quicker. She took the oats meant for Peter right between the ears. Peter's carrot meanwhile hit the killer hard and he went down like a sack of potatoes. There was a mass flight of bears as Peter cradled Lola in his arms.

'You crazy bunny,' he whispered. 'What made you do that? We made our choices, baby. Mine was to never stop loving you, and yours was that rowdy smart-alec sociopath with truth issues. So you got Bugs and I got drunk. And now I'm sober and you're dying. Do you want to say anything, baby?'

Lola's breathing was very shallow. With a last effort, the demising doe lifted her head. 'You stupid big-hearted, big-footed lolloping lummox', she whispered. 'Do you know, I might have done it even if Winnie hadn't pushed me'. There was no point in sending for Archie Ambulance; this was one for Harry Hearse.

The carriage was now bear bare, except for Mummy Bear and Baby Bear hunched over the Daddy. Just another furry story gone wrong, thought Peter; somewhere, a blonde would be in it. Outside there was a hubbub of posturing characters, many of them pointlessly repeating their catchphrases. Peter pushed an incoherent, staggering Postman Pat out of the way as Winnie waddled off into the distance as fast as his little legs could carry him. Loud barking signalled that Lassie had finally arrived, out of breath. Too late. Always too late. Peter turned up the collar of his jacket and started walking back up the track. It was time to go home, camomile tea or no camomile tea.

With great affection and admiration for all children's characters, stories, writers and children; but, most of all, for parents.

ACKNOWLEDGEMENTS +++

My particular thanks are owed to Gordon House for his encouragement of *Lost In The Wash, The Quiet Carriage* and *Way Out South West*; to Flavio Gracias of the Goan Association (UK) for his advice on *Way Out South West*; to Craig Stevens for his expertise and unfailing patience; to the members of that now lost and legendary team, the Berkshire Press XV, for the laughter, the drinks, and the occasional pass; and, most of all, to my beloved wife, Liv, for her artistry, eye, improvements, support and superhuman forbearance.

I should also like to salute the fine composers and lyricists who were not credited in the text for writing these songs:

Adolfo Utrera Nilo Menéndez, Eddie Rivera and Eddie Woods, *Green Eyes.*
Cindy Walker, *Distant Drums*.
Dmitri Tiomkin, Paul Francis Webster, *The Green Leaves of Summer.*
Bronislaw Kaper, Ned Washington, *On Green Dolphin Street.*
Rodgers and Hammerstein, *Some Enchanted Evening.*
Michel Legrand, Al Bergman and Lyn Bergman, *Windmills of Your Mind.*
Cy Coleman, Carolyn Leigh, *Witchcraft.*
Billy Taylor and Dick Dallas, *I Wish I Knew How It Would Feel To Be Free*
Vernon Duke, Ira Gershwin, *I Can't Get Started With You.*
Ralph Ruvin, Bob Halfin, Harold Irving, Johnny Sheridan,
'You're A Pink Toothbrush'.
Paul Anka, Claude François and Jacques Revaux, *My Way*.
John Kander, Fred Ebb, *New York, New York.*
Robert and Richard Sherman, *Colonel Hathi's March.*

19685618R00127

Printed in Great Britain
by Amazon